KU-634-912

SPECIAL MESSAGE TO READERS

This book is published under the auspices of

THE ULVERSCROFT FOUNDATION

(registered charity No. 264873 UK)

Established in 1972 to provide funds for research, diagnosis and treatment of eye diseases. Examples of contributions made are: —

A Children's Assessment Unit at Moorfield's Hospital, London.

●

Twin operating theatres at the Western Ophthalmic Hospital, London.

●

A Chair of Ophthalmology at the Royal Australian College of Ophthalmologists.

●

The Ulverscroft Children's Eye Unit at the Great Ormond Street Hospital For Sick Children, London.

You can help further the work of the Foundation by making a donation or leaving a legacy. Every contribution, no matter how small, is received with gratitude. Please write for details to:

THE ULVERSCROFT FOUNDATION,
The Green, Bradgate Road, Anstey,
Leicester LE7 7FU, England.
Telephone: (0116) 236 4325

In Australia write to:
THE ULVERSCROFT FOUNDATION,
c/o The Royal Australian and New Zealand
College of Ophthalmologists,
94-98, Chalmers Street, Surry Hills,
N.S.W. 2010, Australia

AT SEAGULL BAY

When Florence Williams and her sister Edie inherit houses at Seagull Bay they decide to set themselves up as seaside landladies, catering to summer visitors. There, Florence's daughters become mixed up with two wildly unsuitable young men. Flattered by the attentions of an unscrupulous entertainer, Vicky tries to elope, but is brought back in time. Having learned that holiday romances seldom last, her prim sister, Alice, wonders if true love will ever come her way.

Books by Catriona McCuaig
in the Linford Romance Library:

ICE MAIDEN
MAIL ORDER BRIDE
OUT OF THE SHADOWS
ROMANY ROSE
DOWN LILAC LANE

CATRIONA McCUAIG

◆

AT
SEAGULL
BAY

Complete and Unabridged

LINFORD
Leicester

First published in Great Britain in 2006

First Linford Edition
published 2007

Copyright © 2006 by Catriona McCuaig
All rights reserved

British Library CIP Data

McCuaig, Catriona
    At Seagull Bay.—Large print ed.—
Linford romance library
    1. Seaside resorts—Fiction 2. Love stories
    3. Large type books
    I. Title
    823.9'2 [F]

    ISBN 978–1–84617–832–0

20171465

MORAY COUNCIL

DEPARTMENT OF TECHNICAL

& LEISURE SERVICES

F

Published by
F. A. Thorpe (Publishing)
Anstey, Leicestershire

Set by Words & Graphics Ltd.
Anstey, Leicestershire
Printed and bound in Great Britain by
T. J. International Ltd., Padstow, Cornwall

This book is printed on acid-free paper

An Unexpected Turn
of Events

'All right, all right, I'm coming! Keep your hair on, do!' Florence Williams put down her dripping mop and hobbled to the front door. Startled by the knocking, she'd moved too quickly and caught her shin a painful blow on the galvanised pail. But her brow cleared when she recognised her caller.

'Hello, our Edie! What are you doing here?' She smiled in delight. 'And why didn't you let us know you were coming? And why come to the front door, anyhow?'

'Are you going to let me in, or what?' her sister demanded. 'I'm gasping for a cuppa after the trip up from Oxford, and I had to come round to the front because you've got the backyard gate bolted. As for the rest, just let me sit down and I'll tell you!'

Florence stood aside to let Edith Marsden into the house.

'I always lock the gate when I'm cleaning the scullery — don't want anyone bursting in while the floor's wet. The kettle's almost on the boil so you can take the weight off your feet while I make us a brew. Park yourself at the kitchen table and I'll find us a bit of my lardy cake to go with it — that's if they haven't scoffed the lot when I wasn't looking.'

Minutes later they were gratefully sipping tea when once again Florence demanded to know what had brought her sister to Leamington.

'Not that I'm not glad to see you, mind, but this isn't like you, leaving your Joe to fend for himself in the middle of a working week.'

'Great Aunt Clara's dead, that's what I came to tell you, Flo.'

Florence put her cup down with a clatter and sighed. 'Oh, poor old dear. Ah, well, she was almost eighty, wasn't she? Had to go sometime; she couldn't have lasted much longer. But why come all this way to let me know? A letter would have done, surely?'

'That's just it. There wasn't time. I had a telegram from her solicitor, giving details of the funeral, and saying both of us should be there. He must have found my address amongst Aunt Clara's things.'

'He wouldn't have gone rummaging through her desk,' Florence frowned. 'Perhaps he had the details on file. I wonder what it's all about? D'you think she's left you something in her will, Edie? She was always fond of you.'

'I doubt it. She washed her hands of us after Mum refused to let me go to her, didn't she — although she always remembered my birthday.' Edie smiled wistfully.

'She remembered us both, didn't she? And the kids, when they came along.'

The two women were silent for a while, remembering all the fuss and bother there had been over Great Aunt Clara wanting to adopt the five-year-old Edith. Childless herself and well-to-do, she'd taken a fancy to the little girl who resembled herself so much, and had been indignant when her offer was met with a flat refusal. Even though Edith's harassed mother had had six children, she'd said firmly that she couldn't spare one of them, however good that child's prospects might be with the older woman.

'Anyway,' Edie continued, 'the funeral's tomorrow and I knew that even if I did send you a telegram it wouldn't leave you much time to make arrangements, so I thought it best to come ahead. We can travel down to the coast together tomorrow. I've already looked up train times, so if you can find me a bed for tonight we'll be all set.'

'Of course I can. We'll have a good old natter this evening and set off in the morning. Alf can't complain, seeing as it's a family funeral,' Florence mused, 'and our Alice can see to the meals, so he shouldn't kick up too much of a fuss.'

Alfred Williams was well known for his stick-in-the-mud attitude to life and always took a lot of persuading when anything different was proposed. Florence gave a small sigh as she thought about how difficult he made matters sometimes. Still, as she pointed out, he could hardly object to her attending a funeral. Family was family, after all.

★   ★   ★

The two sisters boarded the train the next morning in high spirits. Once the funeral was over, they'd have a few hours to spare before the return journey, and they meant to make the most of it.

'It's grand to have a bit of a day out — even though it's a sad event that's taking us there,' Edie said. 'I don't suppose many of the attractions will be open at this time of year, but there's sure to be somewhere open in the town where we can have a meal. After that we could have a walk along the pier, what do you think?'

'If it's not too windy. I've got my best hat on — don't want it blown out to sea!' Florence chuckled. 'Any idea where the church is, for the service?'

'Not really, but we can get a cab at the station. The cabbie's sure to know.'

In due time they were sitting in a cab, the horse's hooves clattering over the road as it trotted along at a brisk pace. They arrived at the church in good time, where a solemn-faced man ushered them to a front pew, as befitted members of the family.

'Quite a nice turn-out, considering,' Florence whispered, for Clara Burton had had few other relatives in England. Three of Edie and Flo's brothers had long since emigrated to Canada and another had gone to the Boer War and never returned. 'Do you think we'll have to go back to the house afterwards or can we skip it and go in search of a caff?'

'Better go to the house,' Edie mumbled. 'It won't look right, else. Not that I relish talking to a lot of strangers, but we really have to do the right thing, don't we?'

Florence agreed.

*   *   *

As things turned out it was a good job they'd opted to do the right thing, for as soon as they arrived at the house they were greeted by Clara Burton's solicitor, who ushered them into another room, whispering that he needed to have a word with them before the rush started.

Surprised, the sisters sat down and waited to hear what he had to say.

'As you may be aware, ladies, Mrs Burton was a wealthy woman. The late Captain Burton left her well provided for, and fortunately his widow allowed herself to be guided by me. By investing the money carefully, I was able to increase her holdings which allowed her to live in comfort, with a substantial sum left over.'

Florence glanced at Edie, hoping that her sister was due to come in for a nice little inheritance. She deserved it.

Her mind wandered while the solicitor read off a list of small bequests to various people whose names were unfamiliar to her; a cook, a housemaid and a boy who looked after the garden.

'And now we come to the main beneficiaries. 'To my great niece, Mrs Edith Marsden, I leave my dwelling house, known as Sea View, and all the furnishings herein'.'

Edie gasped. This was far more than she'd expected! A four-storey house overlooking the promenade was worth a great deal of money. What on earth would Joe say when he heard?

The solicitor, however, hadn't finished.

' 'And to my great niece, Mrs Florence Williams, I leave the property next door, known as Stella Maris, and all the furnishings therein'.'

8

Now it was Florence's turn to gasp.

'I didn't know Auntie owned another house!'

'Oh, yes indeed. Property is always a wise investment and when the house next door came up for sale two years ago, I advised her to buy it.' The rather pompous little man looked pleased with himself. 'It meant she was able to keep an eye on her tenants there without appearing to do so.'

'Tenants, you say? So someone's living there at the moment?' Florence asked.

'Yes, but the lady in question will shortly be going out to India to join her husband. She came home until her children were settled at boarding school but she is due to sail this summer, so the house will be empty once again.'

Both women were stunned into silence. They'd come to Caxton-on-Sea from their modest, rented homes and they'd be returning to their families as property owners — and not just any property owners, at that. This section of the seaside resort, which was known to the locals as Seagull Bay, was highly desirable. Summer visitors came from all over England to stay in the holiday boarding houses there while taking in the delights of the sand, sea and fresh air.

The solicitor reminded them of this.

'You should have no trouble selling these houses.' He nodded. 'They will fetch a considerable sum, I know, and I shall be happy to assist with the details according to what your husbands decide should be done with the properties.'

He took out his card case and handed a card to each of the sisters.

'If they write to me at my chambers I'll be in touch. Naturally, they are free to contact a solicitor of their own choosing if they wish, but as I have conducted Mrs Burton's business affairs for these many years it would greatly simplify matters if I continue to handle the dispositions of the will.'

'You haven't mentioned our brothers,' Edie ventured. 'Is there nothing for them?'

'Not at this time, Mrs Marsden. When they went out to Canada years ago, it was Mrs Burton's husband who paid their passage. And I understand that he provided them with a small competence, to enable them to get started in the new country.'

'Well I never!' Florence spluttered. 'They never told us that!'

'I suppose they were told to keep it quiet,' Edie countered. 'And to think that Auntie never spoke to Mum again after she refused to let me go! Goodness me, here I've been thinking harsh things about the old girl all these years because of that, while without us knowing, she and her husband did all that to help the boys.'

She shook her head in amazement.

'Indeed. As Mrs Burton saw it, your brothers had already received their share in her estate,' the solicitor explained.

The wheels had been turning in Florence's head and now she spoke out hesitantly. 'These houses we've inherited. You said that our husbands will have to decide whether to keep them or not, but don't we have a say in the matter? I mean, does the property belong to us, or to them?'

He looked at her over the top of his spectacles. 'Actually, to you alone, Mrs Williams. There was a time when all property, with the exclusion of a woman's dower rights, came under the ownership of her husband. However, the Women's Property Act of 1882 changed all this so yes, once the will is probated the houses will belong to you alone.'

Making a steeple with his hands he glanced from Edie to Florence, frowning at them over his fingertips. 'Of course, I am sure that you will allow yourselves to be guided by your husbands, who will be wiser and more experienced than yourselves when it comes to dealing with such matters.'

'Of course,' Edie murmured, not daring to look at Florence, whom she was sure was about to explode. 'Thank you for explaining things to us, Mr Bassett.'

She ushered her sister out of the room, hissing 'Later!' out of the side of her mouth, fearful that Florence was about to vent some uncomplimentary remark about men in general and solicitors in particular.

The two of them greeted the other guests, sipped tea and nibbled on dainty sandwiches. All the time they were making polite small talk with family members they hadn't seen for years, they were conscious of the fact that they had arrived here as poor relations but would be leaving as women of property.

* * *

'I thought you were going to come out with something rude back there where he could hear you,' Edie confessed,

13

when they were strolling along the promenade later, desperately holding on to their best hats against a stiff breeze.

'Well, silly old windbag — making out that our husbands are our lords and masters!'

'Well, aren't they?' Edie chuckled.

'They like to think they are!' Florence grinned. 'It's all a question of handling them properly! I say, though, Edie, this is a bit of all right, isn't it? Good old Aunt Clara! Fancy leaving it all to us!'

'Well, she couldn't take it with her, could she?'

'Maybe not, but she might have left it to the cats' home, like some old dears do. My goodness, Alf'll fall over backwards when he hears about this. We're going to have a fine time thinking how to spend the money once we get our hands on it.'

'P'raps so,' Edie paused, looking thoughtful. 'But I think I've got a better idea. If I can talk Joe into moving down here I'm going to turn Sea View into a summer boarding house.'

'Never!' Florence stopped short and stared, open-mouthed, at her sister. 'Have you gone potty? I have a hard enough time clearing up after our lot. Catch me running around after a bunch of strangers.'

They'd reached the seat overlooking the sea and Edie sank down on it with a grateful sigh. 'I've got to get these shoes off for a minute. My feet are aching.'

'Don't do that or you'll never get them back on again,' Florence advised, sitting beside her. 'Take it from one who knows. You didn't mean it about moving to Caxton, did you?'

'I did, too. You know that Joe's never been right since he came back from South Africa with that wound. He goes from one job to another but as soon as they find out he's no good for heavy work, out he goes. The sea air will do him the world of good, and if I open up Sea View like I said, he can help around the house a bit, or potter round down on the sands. The money I bring in will keep us now there'll be no rent to find.'

'You'll be run off your feet, gal.'

'That's the beauty of it. Remember when we took young Bertie on holiday to Great Yarmouth? We had to get out of the house right after breakfast and not go back until it was time for high tea. It's the same everywhere with these seaside places. Then, come autumn, we'll have the place to ourselves until the next season. Imagine putting your feet up all winter, Flo; what a luxury!' Edie's face was glowing with excitement. 'I've often thought that being a seaside landlady would be the life for me, and now my chance has come.'

Florence looked doubtful. 'What about Joe, then? What's he going to say to all this?'

'You just leave Joe to me, gal. I've an idea he just might like it,' Edie said comfortably. She glanced at her sister as another thought struck her. 'Look here, Flo, why don't you come as well?'

'What?'

'It'd be lovely, the two of us living side by side, helping each other out. What have you got to keep you in Leamington, when all's said and done?'

Florence pulled a wry face. 'Alf and the girls have their work, that's what's in Leamington.'

'Pooh! Your Alf's a station porter — he can do the same thing down here. Remember the porter we saw hobbling about when we got off the train? If you ask me it's about time they put that old fellow out to grass. He could hardly move that barrow. As for the girls, they can find shop work in Caxton.'

Florence mulled the idea over. Everything Edie said made sense.

'I'll think about it,' she promised, although she doubted if her husband could be talked round. Alf was a man of fixed opinions and strong views and once he had his mind made up there was no shifting him.

'Besides, if we take the money from selling these houses it'll slip through our fingers in no time,' Edie pointed

17

out. 'It may sound like a lot now but it's easily frittered away. Best to use it for something lasting, I say — preferably something that'll bring in a bit of cash.'

'We could keep them and rent them out, I suppose.'

'And us not there to keep an eye on things? We might get somebody who'd keep coal in the bath, or rip out the banisters to use for firewood, or pawn all the furniture!'

'All right, all right! I've told you, I'll give it some thought.'

Florence knew that Edie was right. It was unlikely that unsuitable tenants would be able to afford the rents which houses in such a desirable area would bring in, but one could never tell. Even people with a bob or two weren't necessarily honest. Besides, the sisters didn't want to be running down to Caxton-on-Sea every time there were any problems. No, Florence thought, it should be one thing or the other. Either sell, or move into Sea View and Stella Maris themselves.

* ★ ★

When she reached home that night, she was appalled at the mess she found. The sink was full of dirty crockery; the table hadn't been set in readiness for breakfast and instead was covered with fabric and a pile of paper patterns. Worst of all, the fire had been allowed to go out and the kettle was stone cold, leaving her no chance of a badly needed cuppa!

'What's been going on here?' she demanded. 'I turn my back for a few hours and look at all this! And where are the girls?'

Alfred looked up from his newspaper in surprise. 'They've gone over to Susan's. Something about matching threads, whatever that means.'

'Leaving me the washing up, by the look of it,' Florence said grimly. 'Didn't they realise how tired I'd be when I got home?'

'Never mind, love, you can do it in the morning,' he told her, with the air

19

of one conferring an enormous favour.

Florence glared at him. 'Alf Williams! Never in all the years we've been married have I left a sinkful of dishes until morning!' she snapped, resisting the impulse to hurl some of the crockery at his head.

In that moment she made up her mind. Within the month she was going to be settled in at Stella Maris, queening it over a lot of gently bred holiday-makers. She would still be worked like a slave, but the difference was that she would receive cold, hard cash in return for her efforts, whereas now she had to beg for every copper of pin money she had to spend.

'Alfie,' she said sweetly. 'Put that paper away, do. I've had a bit of news.'

Surprised at her sudden change of tone, Alfie did so.

His eyes brightened as she unfolded the story.

'So old Aunt Clara's come up trumps! I was hoping she might. And you've each got a house, and all the furniture that goes with it, have you?' He beamed at her. 'Tell you what: as soon as the tenant moves out, we'll go down there and have a look and bring a few bits and pieces back here. A nice fireside rug, say. This one's all thread-bare. Any idea what the rest of the stuff is like? In good condition, is it?'

Florence took a deep breath. 'Edie's had an idea,' she told him, silently apologising for laying all the blame on her sister.

'Oh, yes? What's that, then?'

'She's worried about Joe, you see. He's never been the same since he came back from the war and she reckons he could do with a bit of sea air. So she's keeping her house and going to set up as a landlady, taking in summer visitors, like.'

Alf looked a little surprised but he could see the sense in Edie's plan. Joe's health was a problem.

'Not a bad idea, I suppose.'

'So I was thinking — how would you feel if we were to do the same?'

21

There was a long silence, during which Florence held her breath. She could see a light gradually dawning in her husband's eyes as he mulled the idea over.

'I don't see why not,' he said at last. 'Our Vicky's never quite got over that cough she had back in the winter and the sea air should set her up nicely. Yes, why don't we give it a go? If it don't work out we can always sell up and come back.'

Florence gave a squeal of delight. Her first reaction was to wish she and Edie were on the phone so she could speak to her and find out what Joe had to say about their plan.

Had Aunt Clara had a telephone, she wondered? If not, they'd have to have one installed, so that prospective customers would be able to ring up to make a booking.

As soon as the solicitor let them know that the house was truly theirs she'd try to worm the train fare out of Alf and go back down to Stella Maris for a good look round. It might be well equipped to meet the needs of a small family, yet fall short of the standard expected by paying guests. There might be bedding to buy, and bits and pieces for all the rooms. The kitchen, too — cooking for larger numbers would require more and bigger utensils.

She pondered over the best way to let people know that the two houses were no longer private homes, but ready to accommodate visitors. She would have to discuss that with Edie, who might have some ideas. Of course they could put up a notice in the front window — *Rooms To Let* — but surely the sort of families they hoped to attract would make bookings in advance, before they left home? Besides, it would save the embarrassment of having to turn down chance customers who weren't quite the thing.

A thousand thoughts flitted round her mind. There was so much she'd have to organise.

The sound of voices told Florence

that her daughters were returning home — and about time, too! The clock had long since chimed nine, which was no hour for young ladies to be abroad in the streets, respectable though Leamington was. She'd spare them a ticking off just this once, though; she was bursting to share her news. It wasn't every day that the Williams family had something to celebrate like this.

'There you are, girls! Come into the parlour at once, please. Just wait until you hear! Something wonderful has happened!'

★ ★ ★

'I'm not going!' Vicky stared at her mother, reminding Florence of the days when she'd been a defiant two-year-old with her bottom lip stuck out.

'Whyever not? You'll love it there. It's a real seaside town with all kinds of attractions in summer. Many a child would give their eye teeth to go to Caxton-on-Sea.'

24

'But haven't you noticed? I'm not a child! I'm a grown woman — not that you and Dad want to admit it.'

Florence hid a smile. At seventeen, Vicky had a high opinion of herself, but she still had a lot of growing up to do. The rude way in which she spoke to her parents was evidence of that!

'I know you're growing up, dear, which is why this is such a perfect opportunity for you. You'll be working side by side with me in the family business, helping to make a living for us all.'

Vicky was horrified. 'Mum, no! I don't want to do menial work. I just won't!'

'Don't speak to your mother like that, my girl!' Alf's response was automatic but his daughter took no notice. What did a mere man know about it, anyway?

Florence's hands were itching to give the girl a clip round the ear but she managed to restrain herself.

'So you think housework is menial

labour, do you? It's what I do all the time, Vicky, and I'm glad to make a comfortable home for you all. The only difference is that we'll be helping other people to enjoy a holiday in the fresh air, which is a real service, especially if they come from the big cities.'

'I don't care. It's not a real job.'

'So serving in that potty little newsagent's is a real job, I suppose? To hear you talk you'd think you were a Matron in a hospital, or something you could really boast about. Well, you can forget your airs and graces, my girl. You're coming with us to Caxton, and that's that!'

'I hate this family!' Vicky burst out. 'Nobody ever thinks about me, or what I want!' She rushed out of the room and went pounding up the stairs to her bedroom.

'She'll come round eventually,' Alf said, turning with satisfaction to the sports page.

'What about you, Alice?' Florence asked, turning to her elder daughter.

'You'll give me a hand, won't you? It's a lovely big house, and you'll have your aunt and uncle next door. It'll be a fine new start for all of us.'

'Actually, Mum, I don't think so,' Alice replied quietly. 'I'm glad for you, of course, but I'd rather stay in Leamington. Mrs Russell is quite pleased with me and when Miss Price leaves next month to get married, there's a chance I'll be promoted to blouses and skirts, which is a real step up.'

Alice worked in a fashionable department store, and went off to work each morning wearing a long black dress with a spotless white collar which denoted her rank as a Marshall's shop assistant.

'I don't know where you think you're going to live then,' Florence retorted. 'We'll be giving notice to the landlord tomorrow, and some other family will be moving in.'

'There's a staff hostel,' Alice informed her. 'I'll be able to get a place there.'

'And lay out most of your money for the accommodation, when you can live free at Stella Maris?'

'I already pay for my keep, Mum. You know I do.'

'What you give me wouldn't keep a cat alive!' Florence told her. 'Oh, I know you do your best, love, but you are just starting out. You don't earn enough to pay for any hostel. We'll pay you a wage, of course, once we get properly under way, and you'll have the chance to save up a bit for your future.'

Alice knew it was no use arguing. If she'd really put her mind to it, she might have been able to get round Mum, but Dad was quite another matter. At twenty-four she was too ladylike to make a scene, but she sympathised with her younger sister.

'I'll hand in my notice tomorrow,' she agreed quietly, and was rewarded with a nod and a smile from her father.

★　★　★

'I do feel let down,' Florence sighed, when her daughters had gone to bed and Alf was preparing to lock up. 'It's not every day that ordinary people like us get a chance like this but the girls can't seem to see it. I thought they'd be thrilled to bits, not moaning like this.'

'They'll get used to the idea, once they've had time to think, love,' Alf told her, turning the key in the lock. 'My advice to you is to get them working hard at helping you get this place ready to hand over to the next lot. You know, washing down walls and all that. They won't have time for grumbling then.'

Florence's heart sank. It was fine for Alf to talk like that; he wasn't the one who had to spur the girls into action. Then they'd all have to knuckle down to it at the other end as well. She wondered if she could possibly squeeze the money out of Alf to hire a charwoman to assist with the heavier jobs. Otherwise the three of them were likely to collapse before they got very far.

A letter arrived from Edie, explaining that her husband was delighted with the idea of moving and thought he might take up fishing, if there were boats for hire fairly cheaply.

And our Bertie is thrilled to bits, and perhaps you can guess why! she wrote *Ever since we all had that day trip to Stratford he's never stopped talking about his cousin Vicky. Now they'll be living next door to each other, he can't believe his luck.*

He'd change his mind in a hurry if he knew what Vicky thinks of him, Florence smirked. 'Idiot' and 'Mama's boy' were only two of the sentiments which her daughter had expressed.

Young Bertram Marsden was a nice enough boy but still wet behind the ears. If he was in the throes of calf love he'd likely receive short shrift from his cousin.

I want to go and have a closer look at Sea View, Edie wrote. *I know we can't take possession until the will is probated, whatever that means, but they can't stop us having a wander round, can they? Shall we go together? Let me know when you feel like going, all right?*

★　★　★

For the second time in a fortnight the sisters travelled to the seaside, this time with a mounting sense of excitement.

'Do you mind if we go to my house first?' Florence asked, feeling a sense of disbelief as she said it. 'We've never seen that. We can go to Aunt Clara's afterwards.'

Stella Maris was much larger than it appeared from the street. There was a well-equipped kitchen in the basement, and a number of reception rooms on the first floor.

'Ooh, look, Edie, a real conservatory!' They looked about them in awe at the glassed-in room which was furnished with rattan chairs and tables. It overlooked a garden, shaded by trees, and it was certainly grander than anything the sisters had been used to before now.

'Why don't you turn this into a breakfast room, Flo?' Edie suggested, looking round at the size of the room. 'It shouldn't be too cold in summer, with all this glass. The guests will love it.'

'Good idea,' Florence agreed. 'It'll be easier to keep this floor clean too, than have them all treading crumbs into a carpet.'

The second floor held a number of large bedrooms as well as a very ornate bathroom containing a claw-footed bathtub and a wash basin encased in mahogany.

Aunt Clara's house next door was not quite as grand, but the furniture was solid and of good quality.

'I do like this piece.' Edie smiled, pausing in front of a sideboard which reached from floor to ceiling and measured eight feet from side to side. 'Nice deep drawers, plenty of storage space underneath — and these lovely shelves above! I can display the tea-set Mother left me. All those little mirrors will show off the pieces perfectly.' She turned to look at her sister, beaming with pleasure.

'Yes, and it's far enough off the floor to make sure that little fingers won't be able to reach your treasures.' Florence smiled. 'Oh, Edie, I can hardly believe that all this is ours, can you?'

The sisters exchanged an impulsive hug, full of excitement as they embarked on this unexpected new way of life.

★   ★   ★

Even the girls were impressed when, some weeks later, the family moved to Caxton-on-Sea. Used to the two up, two down which had been their house on Falmouth Street, they explored Stella Maris with wide eyes.

Even Vicky's sullen expression lightened a little when she was allowed to choose a room for herself instead of having to share with Alice as she'd done all her life.

Her face fell, however, when Cousin Bertie rang the doorbell and offered to take her on a guided tour of the town; the Marsdens had moved in to Sea View a few days earlier and he already knew his way about.

'Do I have to?' she mouthed at Florence, but her mother simply nodded pleasantly to Bertie and told her not to go out without her hat. This might be the seaside, but her daughters were still expected to behave like young ladies.

Several days of scrubbing and painting followed, and then at last the work was done, and the family had nothing to do but sit back and wait for their first guests to arrive.

Alf had already landed a job as a porter at the station, which pleased his wife because it meant that they wouldn't be entirely dependent on the income from the guest-house. Now they faced a whole new life, one that held untold promise.

A New Way of Life

Alice looked up shyly at the man standing on the doorstep. What on earth was the matter with her? It felt as though dozens of butterflies were jockeying for position in her stomach. Could this be love at first sight? Words failed her.

He had black hair, piercing blue eyes and an engaging grin. Also, he stood out from the other men she had come across recently because of his casual dress; light coloured trousers, a blue blazer and a rather loose white shirt. Perhaps he was some sort of artist?

The vision cleared his throat. 'So do you?'

'Er — sorry, what? I didn't quite catch what you said,' Alice stammered nervously.

'Do you have a room to let?' he

repeated, showing more patience than she felt she deserved.

'I'm afraid we don't take lodgers,' she whispered. 'Just holiday-makers, you know?'

'Quite so. And that, you might say, is what I am. Randall Palmer is the name. I work as a beach photographer, you see. People like to have a memento of their holiday, something to look back on, and I supply them with that.

'I travel about from one holiday resort to another, and this is the turn of Caxton-on-Sea! I've just come from the train station and I like the look of Stella Maris.' He paused and gave her another winning smile. 'I like the look of the owner, as well!'

'Oh, I'm not the owner,' Alice said, wishing she didn't blush so easily. 'That's my parents; well, my mother, really. She's the one who has the say in who comes to stay. She's out at the moment but if you'd like to come back after three . . . '

'I'll do that, then.' He smiled, picking

up his bags and backing away down the steps.

Alice could have kicked herself. She'd made a proper exhibition of herself, staring at him with her mouth open like a lovesick schoolgirl. Of course, he wouldn't be back, but what else could she have done? Mum was wary about taking in single men, and this one wasn't a real holiday-maker, was he?

The Crisp family, now, they were more to Mum's liking. Mr Crisp, with his neat little moustache, and hair which was beginning to go grey at the edges, looked quite dapper in his blazer, sandshoes and panama hat. He seemed very proud of his little boy, who had arrived at the house wearing a Norfolk jacket, bow tie and schoolboy cap, quite the little gentleman.

Mrs Crisp, like most of the other ladies Alice saw on the promenade, was much more formally attired, in a fashionable puff-sleeved dress with fitted cuffs at the wrist. Not for the first time Alice thought that the ladies on the beach must feel the heat terribly in their tight corsets and large hats, and sand and sea water must wreak havoc on the hems of their gowns. At least their little girl had the freedom of a shorter frock, even though Mrs Crisp insisted on the child wearing her long black woolly stockings.

★　★　★

Surprisingly, Mr Palmer did return later, and Alice was amazed to see that Florence quickly fell under his spell.

'The back bedroom is unoccupied at present.' She smiled. 'Alice will show you up, won't you, dear?'

Tongue-tied, Alice nodded. For once she wished she was more like her younger sister. Vicky would have chattered easily and by the time she came back downstairs she would have assembled a whole biography of their guest, where he came from, what he liked best to eat, and who his grandmother was!

'This will do very nicely,' he said when he'd looked around the room and felt the mattress. 'Better by far than some I've stayed in.'

'That's good. Then I'll leave you to unpack, Mr Palmer.'

'Call me Randall,' he said carelessly. 'I never stand on ceremony — at least, not with beautiful young ladies!'

He was just being silly, of course, like some of the men who had wandered into Marshall's in Leamington to buy gifts for their wives or mothers, but she couldn't help feeling flattered.

She would have liked to return the compliment by saying 'and you must call me Alice,' but Mum would have a fit if she did. No familiarity with the paying guests, that was her motto.

In any case, Alice was the daughter of the house, not a parlour maid, and as such she deserved some respect. Miss Williams it would have to be!

* * *

Some days later, after the usual chores had been completed, Alice found herself free for the afternoon. She had been planning to start reading a new novel which she'd borrowed from the penny library, but she'd been working hard indoors for several days and now felt she really needed to get out and about.

'I think I'll have a bit of a walk, Mum,' she called as she pinned on her hat in front of the hall mirror.

Florence put her head round the parlour door.

'That's right, dear, you go outside and get a bit of that good sea air. You shouldn't stay cooped up on a lovely day like this. You've been working hard these last few days, anyway, so you deserve a break. Why don't you go up to the High Street and have a look in the shops? I heard they've got some smart new blouses in at that place on the corner.'

'Yes, Mum.'

Alice had every intention of going to

look at those blouses, but somehow her feet took her in the direction of the beach instead.

It was a lovely day. The tide was out and the long expanse of sand was teeming with people. Barelegged children, wearing bulky rubber knickers to protect their clothing, were playing a form of cricket, or begging to be allowed a donkey ride. Parents were stretched out in deck chairs and uniformed nursemaids were exhorting their charges to be careful.

Seagulls were everywhere, hoping for sandwich crusts which children threw to them when their parents weren't looking. Alice could see why the year-round residents called this Seagull Bay. The mournful cries of the birds seemed to capture the very essence of the place.

A moment later, she spied Mr Palmer — Randall — farther down the beach. At least, she supposed it was him, for surely there couldn't be two photographers here at the same time. His camera was mounted on a tripod with telescoping legs and Randall was bent over the apparatus with his head under some sort of black cloth.

He was taking a picture of four small children who were busily filling in the moat around a rather lumpy sand-castle, but as she approached he straightened up with a muffled curse.

He acknowledged her with a nod, but he looked exasperated.

'That would make a splendid picture if only they'd keep still!' he sighed. 'But the little boy in the striped jersey keeps fluttering around like a demented moth. I've snapped them just the same but it won't be any good. He'll only come out in a blur.'

Alice would have liked to ask why this was but she didn't want to display her ignorance so she simply smiled sympathetically and commented that it must be hot work, standing with his head under a cloth like that.

'You can say that again! I'm as dry as the Sahara. Come on, Miss Williams,

I'll buy you a glass of lemonade.'

'Oh, I don't think . . . '

'But I insist! There's a stall just down the way. You surely don't mind taking a drink with me in public? We've plenty of chaperones here!' He smiled disarmingly and Alice felt her colour rise.

What would Vicky have done? By now she'd be leading the way! In fact, it occurred to Alice that if she didn't give him a bit of encouragement, her pretty young sister would get her hooks into him and that would be that!

Feeling rather self-conscious, she walked along beside him, holding up her skirts as she went. Mum wouldn't be best pleased if she came home with the hem of her dress covered with sand. As it was she'd be wanting to know why Alice was wearing her best dress just for an afternoon walk!

The lemonade was very welcome on such a hot day and Alice was delighted to have been invited to spend some time with such a handsome man.

The interlude over, she hoped that

Randall would suggest walking back to Stella Maris with her, but all he said was that he must get back to work while the light was still good. Feeling rather let-down, she went home alone, reaching the house in time to hear angry words coming from the kitchen.

'Do lower your voice, Victoria! What would the guests think if they could hear you shouting like a fishwife? Nothing lowers the tone of any establishment more than raucous voices.'

'There's nobody here, Mother. You know they won't be back until teatime, and that Bertie is enough to make a cat shout. He keeps following me about, bleating.'

'Don't be silly, dear. He's your cousin. Surely you can be pleasant to the poor boy?'

'Not when he keeps saying idiotic things like, 'I thay, I do think you're rather thplendid, Vicky.' '

'Now don't mimic the poor lad. He can't help having a lisp.'

'No, but he can help inflicting

himself on me. Can't you have a word with Auntie Edie and make her warn him off?'

Smiling, Alice crept up to her bedroom, where she exchanged her pretty, rose-sprigged frock for more workaday garb. Poor Vicky! Never mind, her turn would come. Meanwhile, Randall Palmer hadn't shown the slightest interest in the younger Miss Williams who had waited on him at table. Alice twirled around the room, holding out her skirts like a Dresden shepherdess.

She knew she was on the verge of falling in love, and now she understood how the poets had felt when they composed their sonnets and odes. Why, the way she was feeling, she believed that she could almost produce some similar verse herself!

★   ★   ★

In the days which followed, Alice made a practice of 'accidentally' turning up wherever Randall happened to be. She just happened to be dusting the banisters when he came hurrying down the stairs each morning, and more than once he returned from work at the beach just as she was setting out for a stroll.

Unfortunately her sister also seemed to have set out to get herself noticed by the handsome photographer, although her behaviour was more blatant. Unfortunately for Alice, it was Vicky's turn to serve the guests their food, so she had the perfect excuse for hovering near Randall's table, at the expense of those nearby.

'Waitress!'

Vicky turned slowly in response to Mrs Crisp's imperious tone.

'This tea is stone cold, and can't you see we want more toast? See to it at once, please!'

Her husband smiled apologetically at Vicky, but she was not impressed. She flounced into the kitchen, furious at being told off in front of Randall like that.

'That woman!' she told Florence, who was frying a fresh round of bacon and egg for a guest who had just come downstairs. 'She says her tea's cold. It was hot when I took it to her ten minutes ago!'

'Did you heat the tea pot?' Florence demanded at once. 'Are you sure you let the kettle boil properly?'

'Of course!' Vicky's voice dripped with scorn. 'Anyone can make a cup of tea!'

She turned her back on her mother, ignoring the little voice in her head telling her that she might not have warmed the pot first, being eager to reach the conservatory before Randall left the room.

'Well, just make sure you do it properly this time, that's all,' her mother scolded.

'They want more toast, as well,' Vicky added complainingly.

Florence heaved a sigh. 'Then get on with it, girl; I've only got one pair of hands!'

'I hate all this, Mum,' Vicky whined. 'Can't Alice do it? I hate it when that woman calls me a waitress in that snooty voice of hers.'

'What's wrong with being a waitress? It's honest work, isn't it?'

'It may be all right if you are one, Mum, but as it happens I'm the daughter of the house, and I've a good mind to tell her so!'

'You'll do no such thing, my girl! Granted, Mrs Crisp is a bit hoity-toity, but you just remember — from now on our livelihood depends on people like her, and if word gets out that we don't know how to treat guests with the proper respect, they'll avoid us like the plague. So you keep a civil tongue in your head — and bite it when you have to.'

Sulking, Vicky prepared to leave the kitchen with the toast rack in one hand and a dripping teapot in the other, only to be hauled back by her mother.

'Put that lot on a tray, Vicky. How many times do I have to tell you? Take a pride in your work, do!'

When Vicky finally reached the conservatory it was to find the Crisps rising from the table, ready to leave.

'Oh, we don't want that now,' Mrs Crisp told her, looking as if she had a bad smell under her nose. 'You've been so long about it we can't wait any longer. Kindly see to it that we receive better service when we return at tea-time.'

Fuming, Vicky watched them go.

Randall grinned cheekily. 'If nobody else wants that lot, I'll have it.'

Vicky set down the food in front of him and went off to clear the Crisps' table.

'Is she any happier now?' Florence asked, when her daughter returned with the dirty crockery.

'They've gone. She wouldn't even look at it, after all the trouble I went to. I gave it to Mr Palmer instead.'

'That's all right, then. It won't go to waste.' Florence shot a curious look at her daughter, wondering why the girl had turned pink. Probably embarrassed at waiting on a man, she concluded.

'I don't know why they bothered to come here, Mum,' Vicky went on. 'That Mrs Crisp acts as if she's Queen Victoria but if they're such high class people you'd think they'd go abroad for their holidays instead, or at least stay at the Metropole up on the cliffs.'

'He seems pleasant enough,' Florence murmured, 'and the children are sweet. Don't let it worry you, Vicky. They're leaving at the end of the week, and then we'll have somebody else to worry about. Why don't you go for a stroll on the prom later? Get a bit of fresh air.'

Happy to be dismissed, Vicky wondered if she could persuade Randall to take a snap of her. She could say she wanted it as a gift for her mother's birthday, and it would provide her with an excuse to get dolled up in her best frock. He'd have to notice her then.

'I take beach photos, Vicky,' he told her. 'Snaps of the kiddies making sand-castles and having donkey rides, and young couples out on a day trip. What you want is a proper studio portrait, taken against a nice backdrop. There's sure to be a studio in the High Street. I'd go up there if I were you.'

'But I wanted you to take my picture,' she pouted.

'Sorry.' He picked up his equipment bag and strode off without a backward look. Vicky was suddenly aware of somebody coming up behind her.

'Hello, Vicky, I thought it was you. Do you want to come and have a game of clock golf?'

'No, I do not!' she snapped, and ran in the direction of home, leaving poor Bertie with a bewildered look on his face.

Vicky fumed silently. What was the matter with people? She knew she was a very pretty girl, so why couldn't Randall take more of an interest? Of course, he was quite old — twenty-five at least — but all the more reason for him to relish the attentions of a young

51

lady of seventeen! She just couldn't understand it.

She would have understood if she'd been able to see an interesting little scene that was now taking place farther down the promenade. Her sister Alice was leaning over the rail with a dreamy expression on her face while Randall Palmer, hidden by a black cloth, was expertly focusing his camera to take her picture. After that the pair walked right to the end of the prom, carefully not touching, but very much aware of each other.

Alice was still wearing that dreamy expression when she returned home much later, having received a sweet kiss while they were standing behind a cigarette kiosk, hidden from the public gaze.

★ ★ ★

Perhaps because of her disappointment, Vicky was more clumsy than usual when their visitors returned for high tea. If she hadn't been watching Randall Palmer while carrying a tureen of boiled potatoes to the Crisps' table, the accident would never have happened. As it was, she stumbled over Maudie Crisp's rag doll, which had been carelessly left on the floor by the child's chair, and the vegetables went flying.

Startled by the arrival of several potatoes landing in her immaculate lap, Mrs Crisp jumped to her feet, knocking her chair over in the process. Her careful vowels were lost in the tirade of abuse which followed.

The other guests looked on with interest while Florence rushed in to see what was going on. At the same time, Vicky ran out of the room in floods of tears.

'Really, that girl is more of a liability than a help,' Florence sighed when her husband had returned home from work and was tucking into boiled ham in the kitchen. 'I had to give them something off their bill for the inconvenience. If we carry on like this we'll be in debt in no time.'

'Could happen to anybody,' Alf mumbled. He still thought of his youngest daughter as a child, to be picked up and pampered when things went wrong.

'I don't know, Alf, I'm beginning to think these are accidents-on-purpose. She's said from the first that she doesn't want to help us out here. Perhaps she thinks that if she does poorly I'll give in and tell her she doesn't have to do it any more.'

'Don't let her get away with it then.'

Florence pulled a wry face. 'I don't know what you think I can do about it. If she was ten years younger a good smacked bottom might have some effect but she's far too old for that. If I send her to her room that may be just what she wants. She can lounge on her bed with a library book and leave all the work for Alice and me.'

Alf put down his knife and fork with a clatter. 'Anything for pudding, love?

I'm that hungry I could eat a horse.'

'Coming right up. No, there's only one thing for it. I'll relieve her of her duties here, but only when she's got herself another job. She seemed to enjoy shop work, even if it was only standing behind the counter in that tin-pot little newsagent's. There are plenty of shops in the town; surely she'll find something.'

Alf sniffed. 'If you do that she'll think she's won.'

'Not when I explain that she's got to stump up for her keep, same as back in Leamington. She needn't think it'll all come free just because I'm running a boarding house of sorts. And she'll have to pay more than before, on account of I'll have to bring somebody else in, if only a scullery maid.'

Alf didn't reply, his attention taken up with his generous helping of tapioca pudding.

*　*　*

'How would you like to come with me to the Bioscope tonight?' Randall asked, with a cheeky expression on his sun-tanned face.

Alice wasn't sure if he meant it. What if she said yes, only to find that it wasn't an invitation at all, but just a bit of flirting on his part? She would be so mortified!

'I'm not sure,' she murmured, playing for time. 'I may be needed at home. Vicky is — ' she searched for a tactful way of saying 'unreliable' ' — not always available at present, and I can't expect Mum to manage here all alone when we've got a full house.'

'I've noticed that Vicky can be quite childish at times,' he nodded, 'but that shouldn't stop you from having a life of your own. Look, I must be on my way, but you think about it and let me know at teatime.' He dashed off, whistling.

Alice's heart soared. Despite all her showing off — or perhaps it was because of it — Randall thought of her younger sister as a child! She herself was closer to his own age, probably.

Alice allowed herself to imagine going to the Bioscope with him, sitting beside him in the dark as the black and white images flickered on the screen! He might even put an arm round her shoulders . . .

She came down to earth with a thud. She had a shrewd idea that Mum would soon quash the idea of her going to the Bioscope with the fascinating photographer.

But she *must* go! There had to be a way.

Alice hated to lie, but could she pretend to be going somewhere else, and plan to meet him outside the theatre? She considered this possibility quite seriously but was unable to come up with a tale that Mum would swallow. Back in Leamington she could have pretended to visit a friend, but she knew nobody here yet. There was no help for it. She must approach Mum outright.

As she had predicted, Florence didn't like the idea.

'You know what we've said about you girls not fraternising with the paying guests, Alice. It can lead to all sorts of misunderstandings.'

'It's only the Bioscope, Mum! There'll be hordes of other people there. We'll hardly be alone together.'

'That's not the point, dear. It's the idea of going out socially with a young man you hardly know. I don't know what your father would say, I'm sure.'

Tears sprang to Alice's eyes. 'I suppose he wants me to be an old maid, is that it? I'm twenty-four years old, Mum! Everybody I was at school with is already married. How am I supposed to meet someone if I can't even accept an innocent invitation to an evening's entertainment?'

'Now you listen to me, Alice,' Florence began firmly. 'Your father and I would like nothing better than to see you happily settled in a home of your own, but these things have to be gone about properly. You meet someone suitable, he comes courting, and after a while you have an understanding. Then you start saving for your future, and the wedding takes place all in good time. Those are the conventions, and woe betide the woman who flouts them. No decent man will marry a girl who has a reputation!'

Florence stood back, her cheeks flushed from her tirade.

Greatly daring, Alice blurted, 'Then what if I say I'm going anyway? You can't stop me; I'm over twenty-one.'

'Then you're no daughter of mine, miss!' her mother snapped.

Alice realised that she had lost.

'Then what am I going to tell him when he comes in for his tea? If I tell him I can't go in case I lose my good name, he'll be hurt or angry. Then you'll have lost another customer.'

'Simply say that you're wanted here. And let that be the end of it, my girl.'

Alice went to her room, feeling very hard done by. All she needed now was for Randall to take Vicky to the Bioscope in her place, just to spite her. And Vicky wouldn't care tuppence about her reputation or what her parents would say; she would do as she wished and suffer the consequences later.

Alice wished she could be more like her sister, but she was a kind young woman and had never liked upsetting her parents. She spent a sad half hour in her room, wishing she had been blessed with a bolder nature.

★   ★   ★

As it happened, Vicky did cause a stir in the family, but it had nothing to do with Randall Palmer or the Bioscope!

Tea was over, and Alice had the perfect excuse for turning Randall down when Mrs Crisp asked her if she would keep an eye on the children while she went out to a musical evening with her husband.

'We shall pay you, of course, Miss

Williams,' she said graciously, 'and all you have to do is to look in on them in their room occasionally, and make sure they don't venture downstairs.'

'Perhaps they'd like me to read them a story?' Alice smiled. 'I have several books dating from my own childhood which should be suitable for them.'

'How very kind, Miss Williams. Perhaps you can find something that Albert might enjoy? Maudie is very fond of Miss Potter's books at present, and I'm afraid they are too young for him.'

Alice had seen the dear little books produced by Beatrix Potter and looked forward to reading them aloud. They were beautifully illustrated by the author herself, who was a maiden lady living at home with her parents.

'It's a great pity I don't have any such talents,' Alice said to herself, 'for the way I'm going, I'll be under Mum and Dad's roof for the rest of my days.'

She went into the kitchen to explain where she was about to disappear to, and as Florence had just made a fresh pot of tea to wash their own meal down, she agreed to have a cup before she started reading.

'Reading is thirsty work,' her mother remarked, 'and if young Maudie is anything like you were as a kiddie, she'll want those stories repeated over and over again!'

It was at that point that Vicky bounced into the kitchen. 'You'll never guess!' she giggled. 'I've got a job! I start tomorrow!'

'Oh, that's lovely, dear,' Florence beamed. 'What is it? Assistant in one of the dress shops?'

'No, nothing so grand. Guess again!'

'A tobacconist's and newsagent's, like before?' her father suggested. Vicky shook her head.

'It's at one of those kiosks where they sell buckets and spades and whirligigs, then?' Alice guessed.

'Wrong again!' Vicky drew herself up in triumph. 'You see before you an assistant at the bathing machines!'

'What! You surely don't mean one of those peephole machines on the pier showing things like 'what the butler saw'?'

'No, Dad, stop looking so horrified. It's those little huts on wheels where ladies who want to bathe can change their clothes, and then they step right out into the water.'

'I believe I've seen them, Vicky, but where do you come into all this?'

'Well, Mrs Grier's in charge of them, and usually she has a helper, only Dorothy's mother has been taken ill, so she's had to go home to look after her. I'm taking Dorothy's place.'

'But what do you actually do?' Dad still didn't quite understand.

'Nothing much. I help them down the steps, especially if they're old, and I'm supposed to keep an eye on them in case they get into difficulty in the water. I wear a whistle round my neck to sound the alarm if anything goes wrong, although Mrs Grier says it hardly ever does. The huts are in a

63

secluded part of the beach and the waves never get too high unless the weather is bad — and then of course nobody wants to swim anyway. Salt water is supposed to be good for people, you know,' she added.

Alf Williams was still trying to keep up with his daughter's eager flow of chatter. 'But what's to stop you getting soaked, Vicky? Salt water won't do you any good if you stand about catching a chill. The next thing we know you'll be down with bronchitis.'

'Don't be silly, Dad! I'll be wearing a costume, of course!'

He was still puzzled. 'Like one of them pierrots on the beach, you mean?'

Vicky raised her eyes to the ceiling. 'A bathing costume, Dad! Mrs Grier's given me one to bring home, in case it needs altering or something. I'll go and put it on and then I'll model it for you, all right?'

'Anything for a quiet life,' Alf said, settling back with his newspaper.

Alice thought it was about time she

saw to the Crisp children, so she went upstairs where she was greeted with cries of joy.

'I fort you forgot about us,' Maudie said. 'Will you read this? It's my new one.'

The book turned out to be the author's latest, *The Tale Of Jemima Puddleduck*. Happily occupied in reading the story, Alice missed what was going on in the kitchen.

'No daughter of mine is appearing in a public place dressed like that,' Alf thundered, 'nor in any other place as far as that goes. Get upstairs at once and put some clothes on before someone sees you!'

Vicky was dressed in a short-sleeved red dress decorated with yards of braid, worn over baggy red bloomers. Her head was done up in a matching turban and there were canvas shoes on her feet, but her lower legs were completely bare — and according to her father, this just would not do!

Despite his wrath, however, Vicky

somehow managed to stand her ground. 'You're behind the times, Dad! Everybody wears swimming costumes now. Just go down to the beach and see for yourself.'

'I'll thank you not to answer me back, my girl, unless you want to feel the weight of my hand.'

'I'm only speaking the truth, Dad.'

Alf looked at his wife. 'Can you tell me what all this is about, Flo? Just a couple of years ago she gave us a hard time because she wanted to lengthen her skirts and put her hair up when she made out she was growing up. Now she seems to be going back to childhood. Either that, or she wants to dress like an unfortunate woman and I won't have it!'

'Calm down, Alf. It's as she says, quite respectable. Women are wearing these costumes to go in the water now. I've seen pictures in my magazine. Why, I could wear one myself and nobody would think anything of it.'

'Over my dead body!' he roared,

pretending not to see his daughter's grin. His Flo had an ample figure and would certainly cause attention if she dared to put on such a garment.

Vicky twirled around, holding out the skirts of the offending costume.

'Anyway, Dad, I've accepted the job now and Mrs Grier is expecting me, and that's all there is to it. You're such a Victorian. This is the twentieth century now. Things have changed since you were a boy.'

'They certainly have,' he grumbled. Born in 1860 he could remember when arms and legs had to be referred to as 'limbs' and people put little pantaloons on the legs of furniture to hide them from view.

Under pressure from his wife and daughter he finally gave way and said Vicky could go, but he was still far from happy about the situation.

A Shock for Alice

'Well, if it isn't the delightful Miss Williams!' Alice was gazing out to sea when Randall came up behind her, his footsteps muffled by the sand.

'Oh, Mr Palmer! I didn't hear you coming. I thought you must have given up work for the day. It's been so terribly hot, hasn't it?'

'I suppose I have, really. I was about to watch the pierrots perform. I hear they're quite good this year. Why don't you join me?'

Alice hesitated. Then she thought, why not? What harm could it do? She couldn't go through life like a frightened rabbit, afraid of her own shadow. Why, even Vicky had more gumption than she did. Imagine standing up to Dad like that and — wonder of wonders — getting her own way!

Besides, watching the pierrots on the

beach wasn't like going to the Bioscope. People just wandered along, no questions asked.

'I'd love to,' she told him and, pleased, he gave her a beaming smile.

Taking her arm, he led her across the sand to the place where the performance was about to start. The troupe had a makeshift wooden stage, covered with a striped awning. There were five of them, wearing the traditional clown-like costume of white trousers and jacket, with a ruff around the neck.

One of the men held a banjo and two others had ukeleles. The remaining two entertained the audience with a series of popular songs while the musicians joined in the chorus. Folding wooden chairs were set up in front of the stage but all of them were full, and Randall whispered that it was just as well they had to stand because then they could get away before the hat was passed round.

Alice was shocked. 'But this is how they earn their living, isn't it?'

'Well, you can shell out if you want,' he laughed. 'I'm one of the world's workers, you know — I'm not made of money!'

Alice gasped at this unpleasant attitude but, unwilling to cause a scene, she turned her attention back to the acts which followed, joining in the applause with the rest of the crowd. It occurred to her that her mother might enjoy these shows — perhaps they could come along to one together.

She felt quite ashamed when Randall ambled off, just as the pierrots started to pass the hat round. She noticed that quite a few other people did the same and as a result she donated a sixpence she could ill afford because the actors had done a splendid job and she hated to think of them going hungry.

'No need to look at me like that — I wasn't the only one!' Randall laughed roughly when she caught up with him. 'D'you want to come for an ice?'

'No, thank you!' Alice could be quite stiff when she wanted to, but she was annoyed when he told her that she looked like her mother when she was in a mood. It was true that Mum could look a bit severe at times but nobody outside the family had better say so in Alice's hearing!

She began to walk in the direction of home, although her long skirts prevented her from striding out as well as she would have liked.

'Please yourself, then!' he called after her, but she stuck out her chin and plodded on.

* * *

There was nobody about when she reached Stella Maris; Mum must have gone next door to see Auntie Edie. Alice was just pulling the pins out of her hat when the doorbell rang, and she opened the door to find a woman of her own age standing on the doorstep. She looked weary, as if she'd been travelling.

'This is Stella Maris, isn't it?' she

asked. Alice smiled politely and confirmed that it was.

The woman bit her lip. She was plump and nicely dressed and would have been pretty if she hadn't worn such an anxious look on her face.

'Do you mind if I come in and sit down for a minute?' she asked. 'I've been tramping all over Caxton looking for my husband and I'm absolutely exhausted.'

'I'm so sorry; do come in.' Alice stood aside to let the visitor into the hall, wondering if she was doing the right thing in letting a stranger over the doorstep when it appeared that she was the only one at home. She had heard of burglars who sent in an innocent-looking stooge to pave the way for them to rush in and do their worst. Still, this woman really did look pale and wan and it was her natural instinct to try to help.

'Come into the conservatory,' she said impulsively. 'Would you like a cup of tea?'

'I'd love one, but I'm afraid I can't pay you for it. I used up all my money paying for the train ticket to come here.'

'That's all right,' Alice assured her. 'I was about to make one for myself. You just make yourself comfortable while I go and put the kettle on.'

When she returned with a tray containing the necessary items she found the girl drooping over one of the tables, looking whiter than ever.

'I'm sorry to be such a fool,' she gasped, gratefully accepting the cup Alice held out to her. 'You see, I haven't eaten today and I don't feel quite myself.'

'Try a piece of my mother's lardy cake.' Alice smiled. 'I always say that'll put the heart into anybody.'

She waited patiently as the visitor gobbled down the cake in a most unladylike manner and reached for another piece.

'Now, you say you're looking for your husband, Madam?'

'Yes. I believe he's somewhere in Caxton but I haven't heard from him for some time and I'm so afraid that something might have happened to him. The rent is overdue, and I couldn't find the money, so I spent my last few shillings coming here. I've called at every one of the boarding houses here and a young man next door at Sea View said that my husband is staying here.'

Alice was overcome with pity. To think that the poor soul had come all this way for nothing! She only hoped that she had a return ticket, or she would be in difficulty.

Oh, where was Mum? she fretted. She couldn't be with Auntie Edie or she would have dealt with this instead of letting Bertie land Alice with the problem.

'I'm so sorry, I'm afraid there's been a mistake. We don't have a married man staying here, just families and someone who takes photographs on the beach.'

The girl's face lit up. 'But that's my Randall, surely? Randall Palmer?'

Alice's heart almost stopped beating. 'What do you mean?'

At that moment the door opened and she swung round, expecting to see her mother, but . . .

'Randall! Oh, Randall!'

'Selina! What in the world are you doing here?'

Alice withdrew farther down the hall, embarrassed by the spectacle of a tearful Selina draping herself round her husband's neck. Her *faithless* husband, Alice reminded herself.

She was torn between the desire to know what this drama was all about, and the feeling that it was rude to play gooseberry.

Her curiosity won. Randall Palmer, gazing over his wife's shoulder, received the full force of Alice's outraged glare.

'I can explain,' he muttered.

'I'm sure you can, Mr Palmer, but it seems to me it's your poor wife who deserves an explanation, not myself!'

Alice tried not to listen to the flood of recriminations which burst from

Selina's lips but she felt it wise to stay nearby in case the Palmers attempted to leave before Randall's bill was settled. Poor Mum had taken a liking to him and had pressed second helpings on him at every meal; it would be too bad if he left without paying.

She gathered that he often went off to his work as a roving photographer, leaving his wife behind in their lodgings. There was nothing wrong with that, of course. Many men, including sailors and agricultural labourers, were away from home for weeks at a time and that was all above board. This Selina was probably a bit lonely, left on her own, but if Randall took her with him everywhere that would cost money they couldn't afford.

'There's a train back at ten tonight,' Selina said hopefully. 'You will come back with me, won't you, dear?'

'Yes, I believe I'm finished here,' he assured her. She appeared to take his remark at face value. It was only Alice who heard the hidden meaning.

'If you'll come into the reception room I'll prepare your bill,' she said stiffly.

He followed her, leaving Selina sitting on the hall chair, looking a great deal happier.

'I can't afford this,' he muttered, when they were out of earshot and he'd been given his very modest list of charges.

'You'd better go and pawn your camera then,' Alice snapped. 'There's a pawn shop in the High Street!'

Without further comment he reached into his pocket and brought out his wallet, peeling off a pound note as if he was doing her a great favour. She was interested to see that he had quite a lot of money in there.

'Goodbye, Mr Palmer,' she said, in a very cold voice.

★ ★ ★

Florence arrived home soon after the couple had left.

'Mum! Where on earth have you been? I needed you here!' Alice burst out.

Florence's cheerful look turned to one of surprise. 'Nothing wrong, is there? I've been for a little stroll with our Edie. And I've bought ever such a nice little piece of Goss china for my collection!'

The miniature pots, ornamented with crests and paintings, were sold as holiday souvenirs throughout England and Florence had a number of them on her dressing-table, each one instantly calling to mind a happy memory.

'It's Mr Palmer. He's gone, Mum.'

'Gone! But he was meant to be staying until the weekend at least! I trust he paid his bill?'

'Oh, yes, I made sure of that.'

'But why? He didn't find fault with the service here, did he?'

'No, Mum. He left because his wife came to collect him.'

'His wife!' Florence's face was a picture. 'But I thought he was a bachelor. Didn't he give you that impression?'

'I suppose he did.'

'You can say that again, gal! The nerve of him, trying to get you to go to the Bioscope with him. Just as well I advised you not to go, then!'

Alice went upstairs to change her dress, surprised to find that she was shaking. What a fool she had been, imagining that Randall Palmer was some sort of knight in shining armour when all the time he was a horrid man who left his wife to fend for herself while he flirted with other women.

She tried to lock away the memory of that sweet kiss on the beach, and failed. How stupid to have indulged in fantasies about where it all might have led. Why, she'd almost got as far as imagining him putting a ring on her finger while her mother indulged in a bout of happy tears!

Well, she had learned a hard lesson. There would be no more involvements with the male guests! Mum had been quite right on that score.

★ ★ ★

Edith Marsden soon realised that all the work at Sea View was too much for herself alone. She envied her sister, who had two grown-up daughters to assist her; being a boy, Bertie wasn't much good at housework. He fetched and carried willingly enough, but put a feather duster in his hand and a cat with a fluffy tail would have been more useful.

'But I thought you said you could manage,' her husband said, when she appealed to him for a solution.

'I said I could manage the cooking, Joe! And that's true enough. If I'm cooking for three I may as well be doing the job for a dozen. It's all the cleaning that's involved in looking after guests who bring in sand on their shoes and leave tide marks in the bath.

'I've managed well enough up till now but I'm getting worn out, never having a minute to myself. Then there's getting the food in. Going to the shops takes time.'

'Don't they deliver?'

'Of course they do, but when it comes to fruit and veg I like to have a look at it myself, or they might try to palm me off with stuff that isn't fresh. No, Joe, I must have help in the house, and that's that!'

'I suppose I could nip round with the carpet sweeper once in a while,' he admitted, but his wife shook her head.

'That's good of you, love, but it wouldn't do for guests to see the head of the household doing it. No, what I need is a young maid with a strong back. The problem is, this place isn't paying its way yet, so I can't think where the money's going to come from.'

'We'll find a way, love, don't you worry. I don't want you working yourself into the ground while I sit by doing nothing. You go ahead and hire that maid of yours, and then we'll see.'

He was as good as his word. The very next day he came home with a sparkle in his eye and announced that he'd found himself a job.

'You've found a job! What kind of work is it? You have to think of your health, love.'

'This one won't do me any harm — I've been taken on as a station cabbie. All I have to do is help ladies into the cab and then drive them to their destination. I'll have to see to the horse, of course, but that's no problem, with me having been in the cavalry out in South Africa. Money for jam, this job will be, and it'll pay for your little housemaid, with some left over for spending money.'

He sat down, looking triumphant but Edie wasn't totally convinced.

'But what about the heavy trunks some of them bring? How are you going to lift them without your old wound giving you trouble, that's what I'd like to know!'

'Ah, that's the beauty of it, see? My

brother-in-law's a station porter, isn't he?' He gave her a cheeky wink. 'We've got it all fixed. He'll bring the baggage out on his trolley and shove it onto the roof of my cab — end of story!'

'I can see you've got it all worked out.' Edie smiled. 'Well then, I'll get in touch with the job agency tomorrow and see if they can send me some likely girls to choose from. Our Bertie can take a note down there for me.'

'Just imagine, Flo — me having servants,' Edie told her sister over the back fence later in the day. 'I shan't know what to say to them when they come for the interview.'

'That's easy.' To hear Florence speak, it was as if she'd had servants all her life. 'Ask them where they've worked before, have a look at their references and tell them what you mean to pay them.'

'Sounds simple enough,' Edie admitted.

'And make it clear you won't take any cheek. Begin as you mean to go on!'

★ ★ ★

The next afternoon, feeling agitated, Edie prepared to interview the four maids the agency had promised to send.

The times of their arrival had been staggered so she was able to take her time and to 'have a think' as she put it, between seeing each one.

The first girl was a very superior-looking being who seemed to think she was entitled to interview Edie rather than the other way about.

'I worked in Mrs Laurence Ramsbottom's town establishment as a house-parlourmaid,' she explained, handing over her references, which were impeccable. 'I'm desirous of change because all the smoke in London affects my lungs, and the doctor says that sea air will do me good.'

'I really need an ordinary housemaid,' Edie explained. 'The guests leave after breakfast and there is nobody here in the afternoons.'

The girl's face fell. A house-parlourmaid did housework in the mornings but changed into a smarter uniform in the afternoons, when she announced ladies who had come to call, and served tea and delicate sandwiches prepared by the cook.

'Oh, I don't know about that, Madam.'

'It means you'd have every afternoon off until tea-time,' Edie wheedled. This was unheard of as most maids considered themselves lucky to have one afternoon off a week!

Even so, the girl hesitated. 'It's just that I'm used to working for a real mistress, one who's lady of the house, not one who does her own cooking and housework.'

Edie felt her temper rising, but she managed to control herself.

'Then it seems we won't suit each other,' she said stiffly, standing up to show that the interview was at an end.

'What cheek!' she thought. 'I don't know what girls are coming to these days, I really don't. A *real* mistress, indeed!'

Her eyes opened wide when she saw the next applicant. Ruth Matthews was decently dressed in a high-necked blouse and a well-brushed navy blue skirt, but her straw hat was set at a rakish angle on her head and a tumble of red curls was escaping down her back. And her cheeks seemed quite red; surely that wasn't rouge she was wearing? Edie would have to put a stop to that if the girl came to Sea View!

Worse, she gave poor Bertie a saucy glance when he showed her in; Edie summed her up as a bold piece. If she could flirt with a fifteen-year-old boy who was too shy to meet her gaze, heaven knew how she'd behave with the gentlemen boarders! Still, she'd come all this way, so Edie reckoned she'd better let the girl say her piece.

'Why do you think you'd like to work here?' she began.

'I had to come home from my last

place, Madam, because my mother isn't well.'

'Oh, does she live in Caxton?'

'Yes, Madam, on Fleury Street.'

Edie had a vague idea that despite its pretty name Fleury Street was part of a sort of shanty town on the outskirts of Caxton, well hidden from the more prosperous section near the sea front. Miss Matthews must have read her expression because she said defensively that her mother was a widow who wasn't able to work, and that was why she depended on her daughter's help.

'I thought, seeing as there wouldn't be much that needed doing here in the afternoons, I could go and see to Mam every day, even if I do have to live in here.'

'I can't promise you that much time off,' Edie said. She felt sorry for the poor, but it was a known fact that not all of them were honest. She could see her teaspoons disappearing if she wasn't careful, and the girl's references were noncommittal, saying she was hardworking but little else. Add her bold manner to that and it could be a recipe for trouble. Suddenly, inspiration struck.

'Have you tried the Metropole, Miss Matthews?'

'What's that? The Metropole?'

'A very smart hotel up on the cliffs. Perhaps they would take you on as a barmaid. That would leave you much of the day free to see to Mrs Matthews and she'd be in her bed and fast asleep while you were out of the house.'

The girl's face brightened at once. 'I never thought of that. I'll go over there now.' She stood up abruptly and left.

Edie's eyebrows disappeared under her Queen Alexandra fringe. 'Well, really! No manners at all,' she told herself. 'Good riddance to bad rubbish, I'd say.'

She was surprised when Bertie showed in two young girls next. They seemed to be almost clinging to each other for comfort. Their clothes were shabby but clean and well-mended and their down-at-heel shoes were brightly polished. They were both thin and seemed shy.

'I'm Ida and she's Minnie,' the taller of the two said.

'Do sit down,' Edie instructed, as Bertie leapt to bring forward another chair. They had waited politely for the invitation, not like that last piece, she noted.

'How old are you?' she asked kindly.

'Fourteen,' Minnie whispered.

'And how long have the pair of you been in service?'

'Always,' Ida said, just as Minnie muttered that this would be her first place, if she got it.

'Which is it, then? What do you mean by always, Ida?'

'Didn't the agency lady say, Madam? We're from the orphanage,' Ida explained. 'They usually send the girls out to service when they turn twelve, but they kept us on to look after the little ones. Now Matron says we should go out and get more experience, like.'

'We're hard workers,' Minnie whispered. 'We can't do no cooking but we can scrub and do laundry, and wash up without breaking anything. Or not very often,' she added honestly.

'When did you come to the orphanage?' Edie asked kindly.

Ida looked sorrowful. 'My dad was lost at sea, and after that Mum didn't seem to have no heart for anything. She sort of pined away and died. Me and my two brothers had no place to go, so we came to the orphanage.'

'And are your brothers still there?'

'No, they got sent out to Canada to work. The governors said it would give them a fine opportunity to make something of themselves. Poor little Billy is only four years old. I hope they'll let him stay with our Johnnie. I don't know how he'll manage if they don't.' A tear rolled down her pale cheek and Edie's heart contracted.

'And I suppose your parents are dead as well, Minnie?'

When Minnie hung her head in

shame Edie wished she'd hadn't asked. 'I don't know, Madam. I was left on the steps of the orphanage when I was only about two days old. They called me Minnie because that was the next name on Matron's list.'

'Well, now, what am I going to do with the pair of you?' Ida looked up in hope at Edie's words, but by the pain in Minnie's eyes it was obvious that with her history she didn't expect to be taken into a decent house.

'Can you two make a cup of tea?' Edie asked, after a pause. 'I expect you're hungry after walking all that way, and I've a nice cherry cake in the pantry.'

She showed them where things were, and went to find Bertie. Cherry cake was his favourite and he'd never forgive her if he didn't get a piece.

'They seem all right, Mum,' he remarked. 'Which one do you think you'll take on?'

Edie sighed. 'Poor little things. I can't split them up. I suppose I'll have to take them both.'

★ ★ ★

'You've done *what*?' Joe Marsden couldn't believe his ears.

'Say you don't mind! I couldn't help it, Joe! Those poor little things. They've been together since they were young — it would be cruel to separate them now.'

'It happens in real families,' he grunted. 'Me and our Sid went our separate ways as soon as we were old enough to get work. Orphans are no different.'

'But you came from a good home, same as me,' she pleaded. 'Just think, love, that poor little boy, scarcely more than a toddler, sent out to Canada to face goodness knows what!'

'As I've heard, it's happening all the time, kiddies going out to Canada, Australia, you name it.'

'I don't care; it's not right, Joe! We can't do anything about that but we can do something for this pair. You can say what you like but my mind's made up.

Here they are, and here they stay.'

Joe grunted. He knew when he was beaten.

Edie was almost in tears when she saw how delighted the girls were with the rather spartan bedroom they were to share.

'We've only had a dormitory before,' Ida told her.

'And we've never had a rug on the floor,' Minnie put in. 'Lovely, that will be, getting out of bed in winter and not having to put your bare feet on icy cold floorboards.'

Edie realised with a pang that she hadn't thought about what would become of the girls when the holiday season was over. She'd hardly need two maids when all the holiday-makers had gone back home and it was just Joe and Bertie to care for. She hadn't told the employment agency that she really didn't need help then; she just hadn't put two and two together, which was foolish of her.

'We'll cross that bridge when we

come to it,' she told herself as the girls chattered on, exclaiming over the fact that they had a washstand to share and would no longer have to queue up in a place that Minnie referred to as 'the wash-ups', barefoot and shivering in their flimsy nightgowns.

'You can pretty the room up a bit if you like,' Edie said gruffly. 'I've got a pile of old magazines you can have. Choose a picture you like and I'll find an old frame for it. That'll make the place seem more like home.'

★ ★ ★

Fright made poor Minnie clumsy at first and Edie became used to the clatter of falling dustpans and chairs being overturned. Still, the child was willing enough and she didn't have to come face to face with the guests, so it didn't really matter. When Minnie realised that these small disasters didn't result in a slapping she soon became more confident and vied with the more efficient Ida to get the work done on time.

The only person who wasn't pleased with the newcomers was Bertie. Used to sticking up for themselves with the other orphans, these girls took no nonsense from him, telling him to move out of the way and let them get on when they found him sprawled in an armchair or sitting on the stairs, reading his comic.

'They should show me more respect,' he grumbled, but Edie was having none of it.

'You think they should treat you like the young master, I suppose! Well, that won't wash here, Bertram Marsden! Those girls are here to work and they can't do a proper job with you under their feet all day long. Come to that, it's about time you went out and got yourself a job, a great lad of fifteen!'

Bertie left the house in a sulk. He lounged over to Stella Maris, hoping to see Vicky, but she wasn't there.

'She's gone to work.' Florence told

him. 'Isn't that what you should be thinking about doing?'

'Not you as well,' he groaned. 'Everybody has something to say on that subject! Dad wants me to be a man, Mum nags me all the time, and now those two wretched girls want to chase me out of my own home. Nobody likes me, Auntie Flo!'

'Come now, surely it's not as bad as all that?'

'You don't know the half of it. I wish everybody would just leave me alone. I'm quite content as I am and I'm doing no harm to anyone.'

Florence gave him a stern look.

'That's just it, my lad. You're quite content to sit back and let your mother wait on you hand and foot, while your dad still has to give you spending money. When did you last do something to help the family out?'

He frowned. 'I don't know what you mean, Auntie. Of course Mum gets my meals and does my washing. That's what mothers do! And Dad goes out to work, because that's what men do.'

Florence was aghast. 'Well, you're on the verge of becoming a man, Bertie, and it's time you thought of what your life's work is going to be. I happen to know that your parents were prepared to make the sacrifice to get you apprenticed to a good trade but you couldn't decide on what you wanted to do. Many a father would have just paid the premium and made the decision for you, but no. It's been left up to you, and you've abused the privilege.'

'You're being very unkind to me, Auntie Flo.'

Bertie had a hurt expression on his face but Florence ignored this. It was time somebody told him a few home truths. She knew from Edie that Joe blamed her sister for their son's apathy, saying he was spoiled. Edie had countered by saying that he was their one and only chick, and she wasn't having him forced into a way of life he'd hate. For once, Florence agreed with her brother-in-law. Their Bertie needed a good shake-up.

'I'm sure Vicky would think more of you if you found yourself a job,' she said, with low cunning. Vicky would have a fit if she knew what her mother was up to!

Bertie's eyes opened wide. 'Do you think so, Auntie?'

'I know so. Girls like a boy with a bit of get up and go about him. This isn't just about pleasing your cousin, though, is it? One day you'll want to have a home of your own, with a wife and kiddies, and that won't happen unless you find a way to earn a living.'

She patted his shoulder. 'Now, you think about what I've just said, Bertie, and go and do something about it.'

She told herself that she'd been cruel to be kind — something his mother should have done long before this — and now she'd wait and see what became of it. If anything!

Bertie left the house in a daze. He couldn't imagine why his aunt had been so unpleasant; he knew he didn't deserve that. Perhaps, though, his thoughts went on, she had a point about Vicky liking him more if he found himself a job. He made up his mind to look for one this very day!

Accordingly, he presented himself at every shop and office he could think of. But he was in for disappointment. The greengrocer already had a delivery boy; the cabinetmaker had an apprentice to assist him; the newspaper office had one printer's devil and didn't need another one. Others asked him for references but as he hadn't worked before he didn't have any. He had no idea how to get any when you started out.

He even went to the hotel, where he learned that although they needed someone to work in the bar, they wouldn't take him because he was too young.

'Try seasonal work, lad,' the bar-keeper advised him. 'That may lead to something better after a while.'

'What do you mean, seasonal work?'

The man looked at him as if he was a creature from outer space. 'My, my, we are wet behind the ears, aren't we! In places like Caxton a lot of jobs are temporary, see — just for a few months while the summer visitors are around. You could try dishing out ice creams or lemonade, although I'd say you've already missed the boat. Those jobs will have been snapped up long ago.'

Of course! That was what Vicky was up to, helping out with the ladies at the bathing machine. Bertie had to pass the beach on his way home so he might as well see if Vicky was still working. Telling her that he was looking for a job would give him the excuse he needed to call on her.

His luck was in. Even with her hair in rat's tails from the sea water she looked as pretty as a picture.

'What do you want?' she snapped, as she towelled her head.

'I'm looking for a job,' he told her. 'I don't suppose you know of anything going down here at the beach, do you?'

She smiled angelically.

'As a matter of fact I do!'

He was rather taken aback when she told him what it was, but there was a certain look in her eye which challenged him to do something about it.

'Sounds good to me,' he lied, assuming what he fondly imagined to be a devil-may-care expression. 'Where do I apply?'

Vicky pointed down the beach.

*   *   *

Edie sighed when she heard the kitchen door opening. She hoped Bertie had got over his sulk; it was high time he made something of himself. She'd have to get Joe to have another word with him.

She couldn't believe her ears when he made his announcement.

'Hello, Mum! Guess what? I've found a job!'

The Punch and Judy Man

'Hello, Edie! Want a cuppa? I've got the kettle on.' Florence smiled at her sister.

'No thanks, I've only got a minute. I've left a cake in the oven. I just came to tell you my earth-shattering news!'

'Don't tell me — you've fallen in love and you're planning to elope with another man!'

'Oh, very funny! No, our Bertie's gone and got himself a job!'

'Never! What is it then — chairman of the board of the railway company?' Florence's heart lifted. She knew it was she who had stirred her nephew into action, but she wasn't about to say so.

Nevertheless, it was a bit of a let-down when Edie said proudly, 'Donkey boy at the beach!'

'Donkey boy at the beach?'

'What are you, a parrot? It may not be much, but it's a start. I'm that pleased he's stirred his stumps at last!'

'That's something, I suppose,' Florence murmured. 'What does he have to do, exactly?'

'Oh, you know — taking little kiddies for a ride and making sure they don't get bucked off. Rather nice; I wouldn't mind doing it myself.'

'And he'll have to do a certain amount of shovelling to keep the sands clean, I expect,' Florence said. 'And the stables, too, I shouldn't wonder.'

'Yes, well, that goes with looking after animals, doesn't it? It won't do the boy any harm to see how the other half lives.'

Florence thought it would do him good! Bertie was rather too dainty in his ways for a lad of his age, and he wouldn't dare to complain when his own father was doing the same sort of work with the cab company.

'I'd better get back to my cake,' Edie said. 'I was that pleased, I just had to share it with someone.'

'I'm glad for you,' Florence told her.

103

'I have to get on myself. There's a new chap arriving today. He sounds rather posh — Philip Montague-Hayes his name is.'

'A bachelor, is he? Just make sure he's not another one like that Palmer fellow,' Edie warned her. 'You've got your girls to think of.'

Florence agreed wholeheartedly. Poor Alice had been subdued since the photographer's wife had turned up; surely she hadn't fancied herself in love with the man? She was too romantic for her own good; those novels she liked to read had put ideas into her head.

As for Vicky, Florence couldn't make her out at all. These days she seemed on top of the world and surely that shine in her eyes was caused by something more than sea air and salt water! A thought occurred to her. Now that young Bertie would be working on the sands, would it be worthwhile asking him to keep an eye on the girl?

Florence smiled to herself at the

thought. He'd agree to it in a heartbeat, of course, but there'd be the devil to pay if Vicky ever found out what her mother had done.

★ ★ ★

Florence was right. Vicky *was* up to something. It had all started on a day when the weather was too chilly for bathing, and she'd been dismissed early.

'No point in hanging about in our costumes if nobody wants to go in,' her boss had said. 'Catch our death in this wind, we would. You push off, love, and I'll see you in the morning.'

So Vicky had changed into her ordinary clothes and wandered down the beach, to see what she could see. If she went home, Mum would only find something for her to do, and she wanted to avoid that at all costs.

There was a Punch and Judy show down the way, and despite the cold, a little group of children and parents were enjoying the antics of the traditional entertainment. A babe in arms burst into tears when Punch began belabouring his wife, but that only seemed to delight the crowd. Loud cheers erupted when the policeman came to apprehend Punch.

When it was all over and the crowd had melted away Vicky lingered, fascinated by the man who had come out from behind the tent with a top hat in which he collected such coins as the parents produced.

'Spare me a penny, pretty lady?' he asked, showing a mouthful of straight white teeth.

'Haven't got any!' she said cheekily.

'Then how about a kiss instead?'

'Fat chance!' she retorted. 'Was that you back there, doing all those different voices? It was ever so good.'

He swept her an elegant bow. 'Twas myself and me alone.'

There was something about his voice — if indeed it was his natural tone and not another of his stage twangs — that made her think he must be Irish and she remarked upon it.

'I am so,' he agreed. 'Straight from County Meath to Caxton-on-Sea to beguile the kiddies. And what about you, me darlin'? Do you live nearby or are you a mermaid, come from the sea to lure a poor fella down into your kingdom on the ocean floor?'

Vicky giggled. She had never come across anyone like this before.

'I'd love to have a look at your puppets,' she said boldly. 'I've never seen Punch and Judy before. I come from Leamington and there was nothing like it there.'

'I'd be delighted to introduce you to my little wooden companions,' he twinkled. 'Come round to the back of the tent and I'll see what I can do.'

Vicky followed, guiltily aware that Mum would certainly not approve of this, but what harm could possible come to her here, with people all over the beach? They would be sure to hear her if she had to scream for help!

She was intrigued by the puppets and by their master's cleverness in working their heads and arms.

'Can I try?' she breathed, experiencing a feeling she couldn't name as he stood close to her in the confined space behind the tiny stage.

'Certainly, my beauty.'

He showed her where to grasp the puppets, and how to manipulate them, and she was quite delighted with herself when she managed to move their heads.

After a few minutes, however, she became aware that he was looking at her very closely. She began to feel uncomfortable and fumbled with the tent flap, anxious to get away.

'I have to go now, or my mother will be wondering where I've got to,' she told him in a breathless voice. 'Thank you very much for showing me the puppets, Mr . . . Er . . . ' She sounded like a polite little girl thanking her hostess for a lovely time after attending a children's party.

'The name's Higgins, Saul Higgins.

And what would your name be?'

'Vicky,' she said. 'Vicky Williams.'

'And where can Vicky Williams be found when she isn't talking to a poor Punch and Judy man?'

She was reluctant to tell him anything more about herself; what if he turned up some day at Stella Maris, asking to see her? Then the fat would be in the fire!

'I work over there,' she said vaguely. 'See — at the ladies' bathing machines.'

She immediately wished she hadn't told him that, for what if he came there and saw her in her skimpy costume? She wasn't sure she wanted him to see her like that, but at the same time she was intrigued by the dark and dangerous-looking Saul Higgins.

★ ★ ★

Back at the house, Alice was equally intrigued by the new arrival, Mr Philip Montague-Hayes.

'Do call me Monty,' he drawled,

109

when she introduced herself as Miss Williams, thankful that she'd discarded her apron before answering the door. For some reason it seemed important for her to let him know she was the daughter of the house, not a maid, although he'd soon find out that she was no lady of leisure when she served him with his meals at table.

In his striped blazer and white trousers, he was the picture of a smartly-dressed holidaymaker, and when he swept off his panama hat to greet her she saw that his hair was a pleasing sort of golden brown, like the toffee Mum sometimes made in the winter.

'Will your wife be joining you, Mr Montague-Hayes?' she asked somewhat primly. She knew full well that he had written to book a room for one, but after her experience with Randall Palmer she wasn't taking any chances.

He waved his hand in a languid gesture. 'Oh, I'm not married, Miss Williams. I'm just down from Oxford, you know, and the pater is giving me a holiday before I join him in the family firm. I was hoping he'd send me on the Grand Tour like some of the other fellows in my year but he wouldn't cough up, so Caxton-on-Sea it is!'

Alice knew that some wealthy young men were given a tour of the European capitals before settling down to work, but probably the senior Montague-Hayes couldn't afford it, despite his snooty sounding name. Either that, or he wanted to put his son to work without delay. She murmured something about Caxton being very pleasant at this time of year, and led the way to his room.

⋆   ⋆   ⋆

Bertie found to his surprise that he quite enjoyed working with the donkeys. Most of the young children seemed delighted to be riding, as long as he was at the head of the animals, and occasionally he received a small tip from a parent.

On one occasion, some bigger lads, armed with sticks, wanted to hire the donkeys to ride off by themselves, and Bertie managed to summon up a firmness he hadn't known he possessed, to turn them away. He wasn't about to let his donkeys be kicked and whipped by uncaring louts!

During a lull in business one day, he was leaning on the tethering rail, staring out to sea, when he thought he caught a glimpse of his cousin Vicky. One of the donkeys brayed just then, though, making him jump, and when he looked again there was no sign of her. The Punch and Judy show, quiet now when there were no customers about, was all that he could see, and she certainly wouldn't be there. Perhaps during his dinner break he'd take a stroll over to the bathing machines to see her, he mused.

At the railway station his father was sitting in the shade, awaiting the arrival of the next train. Edie was expecting a new guest, and Joe had hoped that he'd spot the man as soon as he got off the train so that he could transport him to Sea View. Then he could see if Edie would make him a quick cuppa before he headed out again.

The train steamed in noisily, causing the cab horse to whinny and shake its head. Joe got up stiffly and went to the barrier to see who was getting off. The elderly gentleman with the beige suit and the high-crowned hat: he looked as if it might be Mr Barker. Joe limped forward, touching his cap.

★   ★   ★

Alice was feeling thoroughly disgruntled. The new man, Mr Montague-Hayes, had struck up a friendship with Miss Carrington from another boarding-house nearby. Mona Carrington was the niece of the proprietress of Mon Repos and as far as Alice could tell she did no work in the house but spent her days strolling on the promenade, twirling a pale yellow parasol over her head. Monty, as he told everyone to call him, had apparently met her when he was strolling down on the prom and they had struck up a conversation.

'That just shows you what a vulgar person she is, getting familiar with a man she hasn't even been introduced to,' Alice told Vicky, knowing as she spoke that it was nothing but sour grapes. She'd wanted him to invite her out instead!

Vicky didn't reply. She seemed to be in a regular dream these days. One would almost imagine that she was in love, but Alice dismissed this fanciful thought, for who was there for Vicky to fall in love with?

All in all, Alice decided, Caxton had turned out to be a bit of a disappointment. The place had plenty of attractions, if you had time to enjoy them, but she hadn't made any new friends here, either male or female. A wave of nostalgia swept over her as she thought of the other girls at Marshall's, always good for a giggle and a gossip when the supervisor's back was turned.

That new gentleman was easy to please, Florence thought. He wanted her to call him Monty, but she stuck to her rule of not being familiar with the guests, and called him Mr Montague-Hayes. He was very tidy in his ways and didn't leave his dirty washing strewn about his room or drape wet towels over the furniture. He enjoyed his meals and praised her cooking to the skies. He ignored Vicky's silly posturing and treated Alice with respect. She only hoped that the Sextons, a family due to arrive the next week and staying for a fortnight, would be as amenable.

★   ★   ★

'Have I told you that your eyes are as blue as the seas off the coast of Ireland?' Saul murmured, with his mouth perilously close to Vicky's ear.

'No, you haven't,' she giggled, 'and I don't believe a word of it. I've heard about that Irish Sea of yours and it's supposed to be stormy a lot of the time. I don't suppose it's very blue then!'

'Ah, but you're making fun of the poor Punch and Judy man,' he said, putting on a sad face. 'I'd like to take you there, so I would, and you see it for yourself. Will you not come to Ireland with me, Mavourneen?'

'Mum would have a fit!' Vicky declared. She didn't even want to think about what Dad would say or do if she proposed going anywhere with this charmer. But, of course, Saul didn't mean a word of it. It was all part of the game.

It was stuffy inside the tent and she had a sudden urge to be outside, running into the cool waves, getting the salt spray up her nose.

'Can't catch me!' she trilled, tearing herself out of his arms and sliding under the flap of the tent.

When she looked back to see if he was following there was no sign of him. She suddenly felt very foolish. What on earth would he think of her? She was behaving like a child, not the young lady she really was.

'Vicky! I've been looking everywhere for you!'

'Hello, Bertie. Why aren't you working?'

'I am. This is my dinner break. I have to go back in a minute. Why aren't you? Working, I mean.'

'Nobody wanted to take a dip today, it's too cold. I'm going home now. Bye!'

She skipped away, leaving Bertie staring after her. Wonder of wonders, Vicky had spoken to him quite nicely! Perhaps there was hope for him yet.

★　★　★

'Dear Mrs Williams, would you mind very much if I were to bring a young lady to tea?' Monty favoured Florence with a winning smile.

'Why, no, Mr Montague-Hayes, as long as it is partaken in the conservatory,' she said in her most dignified

117

manner. 'Young ladies are not permitted in the gentlemen's rooms, of course.'

'Oh, of course not, Mrs Williams.' He looked indignant. 'I wouldn't dream of such a thing!'

'And pigs might fly,' Florence thought, but of course she didn't say the words aloud.

As Alice could have told her, the guest was Mona Carrington from down the road. Florence knew her aunt by sight but had never actually spoken to the niece although she'd seen her passing by the window often enough.

She'd always summed her up as a rather colourless young woman, despite the fancy parasol, but now, on the appointed day, Mona seemed positively animated, gazing into Monty's eyes and hanging on his every word. Alice watched them glumly.

'What's the matter with you?' her mother demanded. 'You look like you've lost sixpence and found a penny.'

'The way I feel I'd be delighted to find a penny,' Alice snapped. 'My life's as dull as ditchwater, Mum — and there's nothing round the corner but work, work and more work!'

'Cheer up, chicken, it may never happen!'

'It already has, Mum!' she snapped as she flounced off.

'Now what can be the matter with her?' Florence wondered. 'She's not still fretting over that Palmer chap, surely? I'll have a word with her later.'

★ ★ ★

'Vicky, would you like to come to the Palais de Danse with me?'

Vicky looked at her sister in some amazement. 'What on earth for?'

If Bertie had said that she could have understood it, but her sober sister?

'Because I want to go dancing and I can't go by myself,' said Alice. 'At least, I suppose I could, but I don't want people to think I'm fast. I'm sick and tired of staying home every evening, darning my stockings. I want to see a bit of life.'

Some serious soul-searching had convinced Alice that she was stuck in a rut and dull with it. No knight on a dashing white horse was ever going to come and whisk her away, so she had to do something about it herself. She might make new friends at one of the dances, or at least enjoy herself learning some of the latest dance steps.

'Come on, Vicky. Do say you'll come. Dad's less likely to kick up a fuss if we go together.'

'Oh. I suppose I could give it a try,' Vicky grumblingly conceded. 'I can always come home if I don't enjoy it.'

Her brain was clicking over like a windmill in a field. Suppose, just suppose, she could get Saul to turn up, too? Alice would see nothing wrong in a man asking her sister to dance, little knowing that Vicky was waltzing about in the arms of the man she loved.

For Vicky had indeed fallen head over

heels in love with the charming Irishman, and who wouldn't? The black curls, the blue eyes, the delightful brogue, all added up to make a package which no girl in her right mind would be able to resist.

★ ★ ★

'How was work today, dear?' Florence greeted her husband affectionately.

'Not bad at all, Flo. In fact, I've got a promotion.'

'No! What as?'

Alf puffed out his chest. 'You're looking at the new assistant station master at Caxton-on-Sea!'

'What happened to the last one, then? You've never mentioned him before.'

'That's because there wasn't one. Fred Parsons, him that's the real station master, he's not been feeling too well, but they don't want to fire him, seeing as he's not too far from being pensioned off anyway. So they've made me his assistant so he'll be under less stress, like. Instead of him rushing outside with the green flag and the whistle, that'll be my job. He can see to the telegraph machine and such.'

'Does it mean more money?'

'Couple of bob a week extra. But that's not what's most important. It'll save my back, not having to lift all that luggage on top of the cabs. Some of those trunks weigh something terrible, I can tell you.'

Florence beamed. 'And if that Mr Parsons is coming up for retirement, I can see you getting another promotion before long.'

'Could be, could be.'

A thought struck Florence. 'They'll have to take on another porter, won't they? What about putting in a word for our Bertie?'

Alf almost choked on his buttered bun. 'That nephew of yours would be no more help than a babe in arms! Donkey boy on the beach, that's all he's fit for. I don't know why you even said that, gal.'

''Cos I believe in putting family first, that's why, Alf Williams.'

'Too late, I'm afraid. They've already appointed someone. Jack Fry, his name is. A real up and coming young fellow. He's been working on the repair crew for a bit, seeing to trouble spots on the line and that.' Alf cleared his throat. 'Anyway, I'm going to bring him home for his tea some day soon, so see if you can manage a slap-up meal, all right?'

'Yes, of course, but why, exactly? You're up to something, Alf Williams. I can always tell!'

He had the grace to look awkward. 'All right, it's like this — he's a fine young fellow, not married, no old mother to support, and no steady girlfriend. In fact, he'd suit our Alice down to the ground. It's about time she met someone and settled down.'

Florence looked thoughtful. 'I agree with you there, but I think she could look a bit higher, Alf.'

Alf fixed her with a stern look. 'A bit

higher than a station porter like her old dad, eh? Someone more like that Monty chap I suppose?'

Now it was his wife's turn to look foolish.

'If you must know, yes! Nothing wrong with being a porter, Alf, and you know I'm proud to be your wife, but all the same, you've got to admit that we've had a bit of a struggle making ends meet all these years. If our girls can wed where there's more money, good luck to them, I say.'

Alf reached for another bun. 'That's as may be, but I still say there's no harm in bringing young Jack home. If he and Alice take to each other, well and good. If not, then there's no harm done. It's too early to be worrying about our Vicky getting married. She's little more than a schoolgirl, and she hasn't even noticed yet that men exist. Give the girl time, do!'

'That's what you think, Alf Williams!' Florence thought grimly. It hadn't escaped her notice how her younger daughter flirted and flounced around in front of the gentlemen guests.

If she could have seen Vicky at that very moment she would have had forty fits but, not having been blessed with the gift of second sight, she remained blissfully unaware. Once again Vicky was inside the Punch and Judy tent but this time she had gone into Saul's arms quite willingly, receiving one lingering kiss after another without thinking twice about what she was doing.

'I love you, Saul Higgins!' she cried when she was able to find her breath.

'Of course you do, Mavourneen,' he answered. 'Of course you do!'

She was a little disappointed not to hear a similar declaration from him, but that would come in time, she knew. After all, he would hardly press so many fervent kisses upon her eager lips if he didn't return her feelings.

★　★　★

Meanwhile, Alice was trying to talk her mother into letting them go to the Palais de Danse on Saturday night.

'I'll have to ask around and see what sort of people go there, Alice. I don't want you mixing with a rough crowd.'

'Oh, Mum! I'm sure it's all very sedate. They have a doorman there and everything, and I know they don't serve drink, not like they do up at the Metropole.'

'I suppose I could ask Monty to accompany you,' Florence conceded.

'Mum, don't you dare! I'd die of mortification if you did. Besides, I think he's walking out with Mona Carrington. He wouldn't want me. Anyway, Vicky's coming with me. We'll look out for each other.'

'I'll have to think about it, Alice.'

Alice pulled out her trump card. 'I'm over twenty-one, Mum. I'm not a child any longer. If I wanted to I could leave home, and nobody could stop me.'

'Don't you speak to me like that, my girl. You're not too old to get a good smack, believe me. As long as you live under my roof you'll abide by my rules.'

Alice took a deep breath. Enough was enough.

'I know you mean well, Mum, but you have to accept the fact that I'm not a child any longer. You're as bad as Auntie Edie, the way she babies their Bertie. I'm going to this dance on Saturday and if you don't like it I'll just go back to Leamington and ask for my old job back.'

Poor Florence was completely lost for words. Had it been Vicky who had spoken to her like that she could have understood it, but gentle Alice? It was as if a mouse had roared.

'Very well then,' she said at last, 'do as you please, but on your head be it. Don't blame me if it ends in tears.'

She turned to the cooker and pretended to rearrange the saucepans. As soon as Alf came in she'd tell him to extend that invitation to Jack as soon as possible. If he and Alice became interested in each other that would solve more than one problem. They could do their courting under Alf's eagle eye, and they'd hear no more talk of running back to Leamington!

She'd make that young man the best meal of his life, and that would keep him coming back to Stella Maris. As Florence well knew, the way to a man's heart was through his stomach.

Knowing nothing of this, Alice went to her room in triumph. She had won! Now all she had to do was find something decent to wear. She could experiment with different hair styles before the weekend, and get hold of some dye for her old white shoes. Life suddenly seemed to hold some wonderful possibilities.

★ ★ ★

Vicky was beginning to learn a thing or two about dealing with men. Flirting with the gentlemen guests hadn't worked the way she'd hoped, and in fact she realised that Mum was probably right. Throwing yourself at their heads (Mum's quaint expression) only gave them the wrong idea. Not that she had actually been at the receiving end of any improper advances, but she could see how that would work.

None of this had anything to do with the way she was behaving with Saul, of course! He had made it plain that he was in love with her, even though the words had never been spoken, so it was quite all right for her to respond. Nevertheless, it wouldn't do to let him think she was desperate for his attention.

'I'm going to the Palais de Danse on Saturday night,' she said casually. 'I've heard that the musicians are very good.'

'Oh, yes? Who you going with? Some other fella cutting me out, is he?'

'I'm going with my sister. She didn't want to go on her own.'

'The poor girl isn't like you, then? Not a beautiful young colleen who'll have all the fellas lining up to whisk her onto the dance floor, but a sad old maid with nobody to love her.'

He was joking of course, but Vicky wasn't about to allow that remark to get past her.

'Not at all. It's just that Mum's a bit old-fashioned and thinks Alice shouldn't go to a dance unescorted.'

He made no reply to this, but simply nuzzled her neck. She longed to ask him if he'd be at the dance but thought it best not to. Saul could be a bit independent at times. It was best to hint at it and see what came of it. Really, she thought with some exasperation, life itself seemed to be something of a dance at times.

★ ★ ★

Edie Marsden was feeling thoroughly frazzled. They were in the middle of a heatwave and standing over a hot stove was a real trial. If it had just been herself and Joe she could have served something cold, but with guests expecting something solid for their money, she was forced to provide the best.

Then there was the new gentleman, Mr Barker. She'd been pleased when the letter had come making his booking; single gentlemen were usually easy to get along with. It was the ladies who fussed over this and that, always demanding alterations to the menu or wanting cups of tea sent up to their rooms.

It soon transpired, however, that Mr Barker was used to throwing his weight around.

Apparently he had been the head of some London bank before he retired shortly before arriving at Caxton, and he'd been used to ordering underlings about. Edie wasn't sure how to handle him. On the one hand she wasn't used to being treated like a servant, but on the other she had to follow the rule that the customer is always right. If she wanted to stay in business, that was.

Now he wanted his room changed. 'I specified a room overlooking the sea front,' he boomed. 'I wish to obtain the full benefit of the ozone by keeping my window open at all times.'

Edie had no idea what this mysterious ozone might be; it sounded like some sort of cleaning fluid to her.

'I'm sorry, Mr Barker, but you did nothing of the kind,' she said firmly. 'I have your letter here, and all it says is that you require a single room on the first floor.'

'Let me see that!' he snapped, almost snatching the letter from her hand. 'This is what I get for entrusting an important letter to a secretary. Miss Pope has omitted the most important part!'

'Then it's a pity you didn't read the letter before you signed it,' Edie wanted to say, but instead she explained that she'd have been glad to oblige but for the fact that there were no rooms vacant at the front of the house.

'Then kindly ask someone to exchange with me, Mrs Marsden. Surely that isn't too much to ask!'

Edie thought that it certainly was,

but she went on to explain that the two rooms were occupied by a married couple and their twin boys. Neither pair could be squeezed into his room, quite apart from the fact that the family had paid the higher rate for their accommodation.

As he glowered his displeasure, an idea came to her.

'My sister has a very nice house next door — Stella Maris. Would you like me to speak to her and see if she can fit you in there?'

'Very well, but I shall expect a substantial discount for the inconvenience,' he grumbled.

Edie didn't reply. Really, the cheek of some people, she thought as he hurried round to speak to her sister.

★ ★ ★

'Why foist him on me?' Florence demanded, when she heard about this. 'He's your problem, gal, not mine.'

'Please, Flo, help me out just this

133

once. I know you've got a room going spare on account of that lady from Cheltenham having to cry off.'

'All right, but he needn't think he's getting any special discount from me, not at the height of the season! And don't you be a fool either, giving him his money back. The very idea! You can say you've handed it over to me, to pay for his stay here. He can lump it or leave it.'

Florence welcomed Mr Barker into her house with a pleasant smile which belied her steely interior. She kept that smile on her face while he insisted that he be served lunch every day at twelve o'clock sharp.

'I'm sorry, Mr Barker, I don't serve lunches. No seaside landlady does. Breakfast and high tea, that's the rule. There are some very nice cafes in the town, or for an extra consideration I can pack sandwiches for you to take with you when you leave the house after breakfast.'

'There,' she thought, 'that's telling

him. The next thing I know he'll be wanting to stay indoors all day instead of leaving me to get on with my work.'

But Mr Barker still wasn't happy.

'I don't care for sandwiches, Mrs Williams.'

'As you wish, Mr Barker. Now, if there's nothing else, my daughter will show you to your room.'

He looked at Alice with approval. Modestly dressed and with a pleasant smile on her face, she was just the sort of young woman the bank needed. It was unfortunate that he had so recently retired and therefore had no job to offer her.

In actual fact, Alice's happy expression had nothing to do with him or her position in the house. She was eagerly looking forward to the dance and even a crotchety old man couldn't mar her pleasure.

★　★　★

The Palais de Danse was run by a family who thoroughly enjoyed their line of work. They catered to the public on summer evenings and had the rest of the day free; in winter, when Caxton seemed to slumber the months away, they didn't work at all. It was an ideal life.

Mr and Mrs Fallon were excellent dancers and they had passed on their art to their two grown sons and three daughters.

The whole family had a very professional attitude. The younger Fallons had been taught to watch for any patron who had no partner. No young lady was allowed to remain a wallflower in their establishment. No shy young man was left to hold up the wall while more confident men piloted pretty girls around the room. The Fallons would approach lonely people to partner them, giving the impression that there was nothing they would rather do than spend the next few minutes in their company.

So it was that Alice had barely put her nose inside the door when a young man materialised at her side, bowing. 'May I have the pleasure of this dance, Miss?'

And a pleasure it was. Nervous at first, she felt herself being guided smoothly across the floor, even though she wasn't sure of the steps. She soon relaxed and let the music take hold of her senses.

She had learned to dance at Leamington, but not at any academy or dance class. She and her friend Susan had stumbled around, laughing, as Susan's mother thumped out the music on the family piano. In those days the girls had spent a great deal of their earnings on sheet music for the latest tunes, and many happy hours had been spent in Susan's home as a result.

Alice noticed that Vicky also had a partner, a rather dangerous-looking young man who could have done with a hair cut. Who could he be? One of the local lads, she supposed. Her own partner, like his father, wore a sort of uniform, a royal blue suit with a monogram on the pocket, to show that he was one of the Fallons. The mother and daughters wore beautifully-cut dresses in a lighter shade of blue. Quite an attractive family, really.

Animated by the dance, Alice had no idea that she was looking every bit as attractive as the Fallon girls, so she was surprised when another man cut in and she was whisked away by him.

'Oh, this one's finishing,' he said. 'I should have asked you sooner. Would you care to have the next dance with me?'

She accepted happily. He seemed very pleasant; surely Mum would approve?

'I should introduce myself,' he told her, but the music drowned out his next words and she never did find out what his name was; nor could she give him hers, without shouting in his ear.

She looked around for Vicky. She was still dancing with the dark-haired man.

Why didn't somebody cut in on them? It was unwise to stay with one partner for too long.

After their dance, Alice's partner escorted her to a chair, thanked her politely and moved away. An exhibition dance was announced and she watched, enthralled, as Mr and Mrs Fallon took the floor to demonstrate their expertise. That over, she accepted an invitation from a man who had no idea what he was doing and had to keep apologising as he trampled all over her feet and stood on the hem of her dress. Just as the dance ended, she heard an ominous sound of material tearing and looked down to see that the bottom flounce had come slightly adrift from its hand stitching.

'Really, it doesn't matter,' she assured him, although secretly she was very annoyed. It had taken her hours to sew that into place!

There was no sign of Vicky, and Alice greeted her quite crossly at the end of the evening. 'Where on earth did you get to?' she demanded. 'I kept looking for you and you weren't here.'

'I don't know,' Vicky said vaguely. 'Perhaps I was in the powder room.'

'No, you weren't. I went in there looking for you and there was no sign of you.'

Her sister shrugged. 'What does it matter? I might have gone outside for a breath of air. Dancing's hard work, don't you know.'

'I hope you weren't with that man I saw you dancing with. Really, Vicky, you'll be making a name for yourself if you're not careful.'

'And if you're not careful you'll be turning into a crabby old maid. You're beginning to sound just like Mum!'

Trouble Brewing

Edie was having a very bad week. It was so stressful that she would have gladly sent her current visitors packing and taken Mr Barker back instead.

'I'm beginning to think we made a mistake, starting this lark,' she told Florence.

'What's the matter now, then? I've taken the old boy off your hands as you wanted. I thought you'd be happy.'

'Well, I'm not. That Lady Salter is driving me mad, and as for that companion of hers — well! I don't know which is worse, her relaying all Madam's complaints, or that yapping little Pekingese. I tell you, Flo, it's the last time I let guests bring their dogs with them! I let it out in the back garden to do its business and then it comes straight back in and starts to wee on the carpet!'

'But you were so pleased when you heard that a real lady was coming to stay.'

'More fool me, then! If I'd known then what I know now . . . '

'They'll be gone soon,' Florence comforted.

'Yes, and how much d'you want to bet me they don't leave a penny piece for poor Minnie who's had to clear up after them all week? And that's not my only problem! The Potters in the rose room are driving me up the wall as well!'

'They seem like a pleasant couple to me.'

'It's that baby of theirs! It bawls its head off from morning till night, and needless to say that doesn't please Madam! If her Miss Phipps has been sent down once to complain about it, she's been a dozen times. Not that I blame them in this case, mind. The baby howls, and that sets the dog off, which in turn frightens the child, and between the pair of them, the place is a mad house!'

'Poor you!' Florence laughed. 'I expect you'll be glad when winter comes and you have the house to yourselves.'

'If I survive that long! I tell you, Flo, I'm thinking of selling up after all, if the right buyer comes along.'

'You can't do that! You've only just got started.'

'I know, but I can't see things getting any better. The trouble is, I'm not making any profit, despite the fact that the house hasn't had an empty room since the season began. And I can't put my prices up because if they're higher than all the other houses charge, nobody will want to pay them.'

'I should have thought you'd be all right, now that Joe and Bertie are out working.'

'Oh yes, I'm managing to make ends meet, with their wage packets coming in, but that's not the point.' Edie sighed heavily. 'I mean, why bother working myself into the ground for no return? I tell you, Flo, I'm thinking seriously about this.'

'Joe's health seems to have improved a lot since you came,' her sister observed.

Edie sighed. 'That's what's kept me from saying anything to him before now. He loves Caxton, he enjoys his work and he likes the house. Even Bertie seems to have pulled his socks up. I can't say that working as a donkey boy on the beach is the life's work I'd envisioned for my only child, but it's a start.'

'Well, don't make any rash moves. It's never wise to make changes when you're feeling tired and blue,' Florence advised her. 'You just soldier on until the end of summer, and then you can put your feet up over the winter and have a real rest. You can always sell up later if you still feel the same.'

'I suppose you're right, Flo, but I'm properly fed up right now. I'm thinking of putting a sign in the window: no dogs and no babies!' she added, only half joking.

Florence laughed. 'That won't get you far. Most people who spend their holidays at the seaside are families, and they certainly can't put their infants into kennels as you can with pets.'

'I must get back,' Edie said, hauling herself to her feet. 'If I don't, that Lady Salter will have made a hole through the ceiling, the way she raps with that stick of hers if little Miss Phipps doesn't dance attendance on her fast enough.'

When her sister had gone, Florence poured herself another cup of tea and wondered what she could do to help. It could be that Edie was temperamentally unsuited to the work of being a seaside landlady, although she couldn't be blamed for not wanting to cater to other people for no reward.

It could be that hiring two little maids instead of one had eaten into the profits; the pittance she had to pay them certainly wouldn't make much difference, but the girls had to be fed. Edie spoke highly of them and they certainly earned their keep, Florence knew, but that didn't alter the basic problem.

But Florence had grown used to having her sister living close by again. It was lovely to be able to pop in and out of each other's homes for a chat and a moan. She hoped that Edie would think twice about her plan to sell up.

★ ★ ★

Strangely enough, it was Florence who, before very long, had to consider getting rid of Stella Maris, although the circumstances were quite different from Edie's financial worries.

Mr Barker had been with them for a fortnight now, and should have been leaving on the Friday, so she was surprised when he asked if he could stay on. He had been a difficult guest but she had taken his whims and fancies in her stride and evidently he felt pleased with the service he had received.

'As it happens, we have just received a cancellation,' she told him. 'I'm afraid we can only extend your accommodation by another week, but if that is agreeable to you . . . '

'As long as I can have the same room,' he said graciously.

Florence nodded. 'That will be quite in order, Mr Barker.' It would mean a bit of shuffling around, but she could manage that.

The week passed uneventfully, and when, on the following Friday, he asked if he could speak to her in the parlour, she assumed that he was about to ask for another extension. Flattering as this was, however, she would have to say no because they were fully booked for the rest of the month.

'I have greatly enjoyed my stay here, Mrs Williams,' he began, with a gracious smile, 'and have found the service to be of an acceptably high standard.'

'Thank you, Mr Barker,' Florence

replied. 'I'm glad you're satisfied. We aim to please.'

'Yes, indeed. I think that you and I suit each other very well, Mrs Williams, which is why I have a proposition for you.'

'Oh, yes?' Florence cast her eyes around the room, looking for a way of escape if it should be necessary. A proposition! What on earth was the old boy talking about?

'I believe that you and I could come to a permanent living arrangement, my dear Mrs Williams. I can assure you that you would not be the loser by it.'

Florence drew herself up to her full five feet, four inches and looked him straight in the eye.

'I am a married woman, Mr Barker!' She would have liked to add a few choice words, among which 'shame on you' would have been the most polite, but he was standing between her and the door, blocking the exit, and she didn't want to get him worked up.

'I am aware of that,' he told her, 'and

your reticence does you credit. Rest assured that I shall speak to your husband about this. Naturally his wishes must be considered before any move is made.'

As soon as he had gone for his walk on the promenade, swinging his Malacca-cane as he went, she flew round to Sea View, where she found Edie rolling out pastry for jam tarts.

'You'll never guess what's happened, Edie!'

'Something exciting, by the look of your face!'

'No! It's old Barker. He's just made me a proposition of sorts.'

'What! Don't be silly, Flo. What would he want with you at your age? Or his, come to that?'

'I'm not that old!' Florence protested. 'And I'm not being silly. That was the word he used. He came right out with it: 'I have a proposition for you,' he said. He says he wants us to have a permanent living arrangement. He wants me to be his mistress!'

Edie threw back her head and laughed. 'Mistress, my foot! He probably wants to stay on permanently, that's all.'

'But I don't take year-round boarders!'

'Perhaps not, but he doesn't know that, does he? Oh, Flo — you've given me the best laugh I've had all week!'

The whole episode left Florence feeling extremely flustered. She couldn't wait for Alf to come home to deal with Mr Barker. She rather dreaded the scene that would ensue when he found out what had taken place. Alf was slow to lose his temper, but on the rare occasions when he did, watch out! The old boy was likely to be on the receiving end of a thick ear, and then where would they be?

Alf would be had up in court for assaulting a guest, and she would be disgraced. People would say that Alf was within his rights to come to the defence of his wife, of course, but what about her? No smoke without fire, that's what people would think!

★   ★   ★

Alice and Vicky were so delighted with their evening at the Palais de Danse that wild horses would not have prevented them from going back there the following Saturday.

Alice was hoping she might see her pleasant dancing partner again. If he turned up again and made a beeline for her, surely it could only mean that he was interested in getting to know her better?

Vicky of course had a different motive. She already knew how Saul felt, and being at the dance with him was a way of going public without her parents finding out.

What she didn't realise was that a girl as pretty as she was could not go unnoticed, and that being the case, it was blatantly obvious that she was spending all her time with the same man.

Alice certainly noticed. Glancing round the room to see if there was any sign of the man she was waiting for herself, she saw to her annoyance that the gypsyish man had turned up again and was propelling Vicky around the dance floor. Vicky was gazing up at him with an infatuated expression on her face and he was smiling back at her in a very self-satisfied manner, obviously relishing the girl's devotion.

Well, it was a public event; Vicky could hardly refuse to dance when she was asked, but still, there was something about the situation which made Alice uneasy. Was it time to intervene?

A thin man wearing horn-rimmed spectacles claimed Alice for the next dance and she was unable to act at once. Vicky and the 'gypsy' were in each other's arms again, and when they danced past, Alice frowned heavily at her sister, who simply tossed her head by way of reply.

When yet another dance began and the couple were still together, Alice knew it was time to act. If she left it until the interval they might disappear into the night, with disastrous results.

But what could she do? If she attempted to separate them Vicky was quite capable of making a scene and Alice could hardly drag her sister off the dance floor, kicking and screaming.

She went over to the refreshments table and tapped one of the Fallon brothers on the arm. 'Excuse me, I was wondering . . . '

He swung round with a professional smile. 'Oh, is it the 'ladies' excuse-me'? I must have missed the announcement.'

'Oh, no, it isn't.' Alice felt herself blushing. 'It's just that I need help. It's my sister, you see. She seems to have got herself involved with somebody who I'm sure is quite unsuitable. I thought perhaps you could cut in and give her a chance to get away from him.'

'Say no more, miss.' She watched as he glided over to Vicky and tapped the man on the shoulder. The couple paused. Words were exchanged, and

Vicky's partner raised his fist as if to start a fight.

Fallon shrugged and backed away, and returned to Alice's side.

'I'm sorry, Miss. Neither of them was willing to give way. I could have knocked him down, of course, but that wouldn't be good for business unless someone was really behaving improperly.'

'No, I see that.' Alice sighed. 'Thank you for trying, anyway.'

He nodded and walked away, obviously wanting to distance himself from the situation, and she could hardly blame him.

Alice crossed the floor and sat down behind the potted palm where she was almost hidden from view. She needed time to think. As far as she was concerned, the evening was spoiled. The man she had hoped to see again hadn't turned up, and now Vicky was making an exhibition of herself.

She longed to go home, but what would happen if she did? Mum would want to know what had taken place, and why she hadn't brought Vicky home with her. If she explained why, Dad would rush down to the dance hall like a terrier after a rat, and then there would be trouble!

Caught in the middle, she felt extremely cross. Vicky had no right to put her in this position. Alice didn't want to tell tales at home, and yet she felt responsible for her foolish little sister.

Meanwhile, Vicky was having the time of her life. She was at the giddy stage of love where she wanted to parade her prize in front of the whole world, and never mind the consequences. It would be lovely to show him off at home, and then she'd be free to talk about him whenever she wanted to, 'Saul says this,' and, 'Saul thinks that,' instead of having to watch her tongue.

Deep down, reason told her that the mother and father of all rows would erupt if Florence and Alf knew about her deepening relationship with Saul.

'We know nothing about him,' her mother would caution. 'A Punch and Judy man!' her father would scoff. 'What on earth are you thinking about, my girl?'

This was so unfair! What was wrong with giving a little entertainment which brought pleasure to others? And as for working at the beach, so did she! And her parents had nothing but praise for Cousin Bertie, who worked as a donkey boy, of all things! Why did parents have to be so stuffy?

'Shall I walk you home, Mavourneen?' Saul had steered Vicky outside as their dance ended and was now whispering in her ear.

'I have to go home with my sister,' she pouted. 'You've no idea what my parents are like, Saul. They're so protective, anyone would think I'm still a child!'

'Ah, she doesn't know where we are,' he murmured. 'She's still inside, dancing the night away. If we slip off now she'll never know we've gone until it's too late to catch up with us.'

'I really wish we could, Saul, but I daren't risk it. She's sure to tell on me.'

At that moment Alice made her way round the side of the building, having just managed to escape from her partner by saying that her feet hurt. She was greatly relieved to see that Vicky was close by, although she certainly didn't approve of what she was up to. To use a vulgar expression, the two of them were in a clinch!

Telling herself that she had to act carefully she pasted a smile on her face and walked right up to them.

'Vicky! I wondered where you'd got to. Aren't you going to introduce me to your friend?'

Vicky scowled. 'Saul Higgins, Alice Williams.'

Alice put out her hand but instead of shaking it Saul raised it to his lips.

'I'm delighted to meet Vicky's beautiful sister, so I am!' He smiled at her, a most attractive smile, and his blue eyes sparkled with mischief and life.

This threw Alice into a state of confusion. She had expected the man to back away, making some excuse to leave, but instead he had stood his ground. He was certainly a charmer.

She frowned at Vicky, who muttered something about having a headache and needing air after the stuffiness of the dance hall. This gave Alice the opening she needed.

'Yes, it was hot in there. I'm sorry to hear about your headache. We'd better get you home at once and ask Mum to find you something for that.'

Vicky knew when she was beaten. 'All right. Saul, I'd better be going. Shall I see you tomorrow?'

'Anything is likely to happen in this beautiful world of ours,' he said lightly, and he turned and walked away.

Vicky was furious. 'You did that on purpose, Alice Williams! You knew I wanted to spend time with him, and now you've driven him away.'

'And not before time, by what I saw tonight! You've made an exhibition of yourself, dancing every dance with him. I'm sure everyone was looking at you.'

'And I'm sure they weren't! Stop treating me like a baby, or I shan't come out with you again!'

'I shan't want you to, if you mean to keep showing me up like you did tonight.'

'I know what your trouble is,' Vicky hissed, glaring at Alice through narrowed eyes. 'You're jealous, aren't you? Jealous because I've found someone special and you haven't.'

'That's not true.'

'Oh, no? What about that chap you were with last time? That's why you kept watching the door all evening, isn't it? You hoped he was coming here again tonight and he didn't turn up!'

Poor Alice was mortified. Of course that was what she'd been doing, but she hadn't realised it was so obvious. So all the time she'd been keeping her eye on Vicky, her sister had been doing the same to her!

This was by far the worst row the

pair had ever had, and it clearly wouldn't be resolved any time soon. There was just too much at stake for both of them.

★　★　★

Making the bed in Monty's room the following morning, Alice experienced a pang of disappointment. The only eligible bachelor within miles, and he hadn't so much as looked in her direction, other than to ask for more butter!

Not that she really fancied him, but a spark of interest — even a little flirtation — would have gone a long way to make up for her previous disappointments.

Taking her duster from her apron pocket, she turned her attention to the chest of drawers on which stood several photographs in silver frames. One was a studio portrait of an elegant lady, whom she guessed was Monty's mother. Another showed a group of young men in cricketing gear; probably a reminder of his university days. The third was a view of a very large, ivy-covered house. Was this his family home?

Alice frowned. Why would anyone bring this lot along on a seaside holiday? It might be different if you were moving into a boarding house for a long stay when you displayed them as a link with home, but here it seemed rather extreme.

It looked as if Monty was trying to make a statement, but who could he be trying to impress?

After her experience with Randall Palmer, Alice was beginning to wonder if Monty was a fraud; she hoped he wasn't planning to skip out leaving his bill unpaid.

But everything pointed to the fact that he was all he claimed to be. His upper class accent, his clothing bearing the labels of top London tailors. Even the book on the bedside cabinet, which was too difficult for Alice to understand when she glanced at a few pages, obviously belonged to an educated person.

She came to the conclusion, then, that he was nothing more than a snob. *Nouveau riche*, she sniffed, having come across the term in one of her novels from the library. She gave the furniture a few half-hearted flicks with her duster and wandered downstairs.

★ ★ ★

The day promised to be hot, and an unusually large number of ladies had turned up to use the bathing machines, some of them with young children. Vicky was trying to persuade one small boy that he must wait until his mother was ready before entering the water when she caught sight of her red-faced employer sending her urgent signals. She waved back, pointing down at the child, and received an answering cry of 'Tell you later.'

It was quite some time before she was able to go to Mrs Grier and ask what she wanted.

'That Punch and Judy man was here again, Vicky. I've told you before I don't want him hanging about anywhere near the machines. Some of my ladies is *real* ladies. They don't want no men seeing them in their costumes. If you don't warn him off good and proper, I shall have to do something about it!'

'What did he want?' Vicky wondered, not bothering to think about what Mrs Grier might do next.

'You may well ask! How do I know what the fool wants you for? I just wish he'd get on with his work and let me get on with mine! And no, before you ask, you cannot go running over there to see what he has in mind. I don't pay you to run after chaps as is no better than they should be, and your mother would agree with me, I'm sure!'

Fuming, Vicky went back to work, and it wasn't until her lunch-break that she was able to race down the beach in search of Saul.

She found him lounging in a deck

chair, a pork pie in his hand, his face grumpy.

'You took your time!' he groused. 'That's twice I've been over there and you wouldn't talk to me.'

'I couldn't. I've told you what she's like. Anyway I'm here now, so you can tell me what's so urgent.'

'I've decided it's time for me to move on,' he mumbled through a mouthful of pastry.

For a long moment Vicky thought she was going to faint, but she managed to hold herself together.

'But why?' she cried, when the world had stopped spinning.

'Things is getting too hot for me here, Mavourneen. I saw the way your sister looked at us the other night. Any minute now she might tell your old man, and what then? What if he sends the coppers after me, tell me that!'

'But we've done nothing wrong!' Vicky wanted to add that two people in love shouldn't be prevented from seeing each other but she managed to hold her tongue. If she irritated Saul, he might leave in a huff.

'Of course we haven't, but what do you suppose the punters will think if they see the flat-foots pounding down the beach after the poor Punch and Judy man? No smoke without fire, they'll say. Better not let the kiddies get corrupted. They might hear something they hadn't bargained for coming out of Punch's mouth, too! Couldn't have that, could we?'

Despite her anguish, Vicky had to laugh.

Seeing her bright face he pulled her closer to him, but she turned her head away so that his kiss landed on her cheek. Much as she loved him, she drew the line at pork-pie-flavoured kisses!

'So this is what I came to say, Mavourneen. I'm leaving on the night train. Come with me, won't you?'

Vicky was astounded. 'Come with you? But, Saul, I can't! What would Mum say?'

'Ah, there's the rub! Are you just a little girl who has to obey her mammy, or a grown woman who will follow her man to the ends of the earth?'

'Well, I don't know . . . '

'Look, you give it some thought. I'll be at the station half an hour before the train goes. If you want to come with me, you know what to do. If not . . . well, it's been nice knowing you, Miss Vicky.'

They parted company, unaware that Bertie was watching them from farther down the beach. He was in the act of leading one of the donkeys along the prescribed route. Fancy was plodding along with a fat boy on her back, someone who evidently fancied himself as a cowboy because he suddenly dug his heels into the poor animal's sides and shouted 'giddy up!' in a loud voice.

Startled, Fancy deposited the awful boy on the sand and galloped away, with Bertie still desperately hanging on to the leading rein. Bertie had never known her to move so fast!

Finally she slowed to a stop, leaving him to stare ruefully at his reddened hands — he'd have a fine set of blisters by morning.

By the time he returned to the stand, to endure the wrath of the young cowboy's father, Vicky and the Punch and Judy man were nowhere to be seen. Bertie was now convinced the pair of them were up to no good. He was disappointed in Vicky. Fancy kissing a strange man, in broad daylight, in full view of everyone on the beach! What on earth would Auntie Flo have to say if she knew?

Still shocked by his headlong flight down the beach, he blinked back a tear. His lovely Vicky! How could she behave in such a way? If only he could have heard what they were saying he might have known what to do. He needed to talk to someone about what he'd seen. He was used to going to his mother in times of trouble, but perhaps that wasn't such a good idea now. She would only tell him he should tell Auntie Flo.

Then a solution occurred to him. He'd become quite friendly with their little maid, Ida. He could talk to her — swearing her to secrecy, of course. Having been brought up in an orphanage she knew a bit about life, and her down-to-earth common sense usually stood her in good stead. Yes, that's what he would do.

Comforted, he stepped forward to assist another small customer into the saddle.

⋆ ⋆ ⋆

'A bit of all right, is he?' Ida inquired when he'd poured out his fears to her after tea.

'I wouldn't say that, not at all,' Bertie replied, looking worried. 'In fact, I suspect he's a wrong 'un.'

'Oh, Bertie, you are funny.' She grinned. 'I meant, is he good looking? Attractive to women, that sort of thing?'

'How should I know what girls find

attractive?' he grumbled. Obviously he wasn't the type himself, or Vicky might have turned to him instead of that chap at the beach.

'Let's say he is, then, seeing as they're all over each other, not caring who sees them,' Ida said. 'I'd say you've something to worry about, Bertie, and you'd better speak to the mistress, and pronto! There was a girl at the orphanage, just fifteen, she was. She was like that with the butcher boy. The next thing we knew, she caught scarlet fever and had to leave. Goodness knows what happened to her after that.'

Bertie was puzzled. 'You mean you can get scarlet fever from kissing?'

Ida gave a peal of laughter.

'No, silly, she was in Trouble!'

Bertie felt he was missing something here. 'That's all very interesting, Ida, but that doesn't help me now, does it? Should I do something about it, or what?'

Ida was no longer laughing. 'I've told you, Bertie, you should tell your mum, and be quick about it. Your Vicky's been brought up soft, see, not like us in the orphanage, who knows what's what. P'raps she's been taken in by this chap. I bet he's promising her the moon, and she's silly enough to fall for it. Let's just hope *she* doesn't fall for something she's not expecting an' all!'

She gazed at him earnestly, and he smiled back at her.

'Thanks, Ida. I'll go and find Mum right now.'

Ida was right. Mum would know what to do. Suddenly a weight was taken off his shoulders.

He headed off in search of his mother right away.

Edie was lying on the sofa with her feet up. She was wearing a facial mask made from white of egg and had a slice of cucumber covering each eyelid. Her son stopped short at the sight. Women were very much a mystery to him and this sight did nothing to dispel the notion that they were a race apart.

'Whoever you are, go away!' Edie

mumbled. The egg white had only just begun to pull at her skin and she didn't want it to crack.

Bertie stayed where he was as if rooted to the spot. Fortunately Ida had followed him in, anxious not to miss a minute of the drama.

'Don't dither, Bertie! Tell your mum what we come to say.'

In his agitation Bertie began to stutter and after listening to this for a moment Ida became exasperated and pushed him out of the way.

'We ain't got all night! You'd better let me tell it.' She turned to face the recumbent figure and took a deep breath. 'It's Miss Vicky, Madam. She's going to elope with a chap she met down at the beach. If we don't do something soon, it'll be too late!'

This exaggerated version brought her mistress into an upright position in a hurry. 'What did you say, Ida?' Edie fumbled to removed a cucumber slice which had fallen under her collar. 'This isn't true, is it, Bertie?'

'It might be, Mum. I mean, they've been hugging and kissing all over the place so I know something's going on. Ida shouldn't have said they're going to run off together, though — I've no way of knowing what their plans are.'

'Oh, lor', if it isn't one thing it's another. You run next door, Ida, and get my sister round here immediately. She'll want to get to the bottom of this, quick! Look sharp now!'

But when Ida returned it was Alice who came with her.

'What's up, Auntie? Ida said it was urgent.'

'It is! It's very urgent,' said Edie. 'But it's your mother I need. Where is she?'

'Gone to the High Street, I think,' said Alice. 'She found a knitting pattern in her magazine and she's gone to see if she can match the wool for it.'

'Yes, well, never mind all that!' Edie interrupted. 'Bertie here says he's seen your Vicky on the beach with a strange man, misbehaving herself.'

'With the Punch and Judy man!' Ida chipped in.

'Oh, no, not him again!' Alice gasped.

'What? You mean you knew something about this and you didn't tell your Ma? What were you thinking, Alice Williams?' Edie's voice was raised and Bertie could see that storm clouds were gathering.

'I didn't know what to do, Auntie,' Alice explained desperately. 'As far as I knew it was just a question of her having a few too many dances with the man when we went to the Palais de Danse. It was silly, and I told her so, but there's no crime in it, is there?'

'Not unless it leads to something more, but you should have come straight home and told your Ma what you'd seen. Nipped it in the bud, so to speak!' Edie snapped at her niece, then her gaze softened a little. 'I supposed you held your tongue in case your dad stopped you going there again?'

Alice felt her cheeks going red. This was too close to the truth for comfort.

'You can't blame it all on Alice,' Bertie piped up, and his cousin sent him a grateful look. 'I mean, if she's been meeting him at the beach, how was Alice supposed to know? They both work down there. She doesn't.'

Edie turned back to Alice. 'Well, what can we do about it now that we *do* know? Is it as bad as we think? What do we know about the fellow, anyway?'

'Well, as Ida says, he works on the beach and I suppose Vicky must have met him there. His name is Saul Higgins, and he sounds Irish to me,' Alice told them. 'He's quite charming, with his Irish blarney. I can see why Vicky might be fascinated by him,' she added honestly. 'But all the same . . . '

Edie nodded.

'I can understand why you wanted to cover up for her, Alice. Sisters have to stick together, but not when keeping silent could lead one into danger. You must see that,' she said. 'Your parents will have to be told, and we'll pray that nothing worse has happened other than

174

a few kisses and compliments. If she was my daughter she'd be locked in her room on bread and water until she came to her senses, and I doubt if Flo will disagree with me.'

'Does Dad have to know about this, Auntie? You haven't seen him blow up when he's upset. Couldn't you go down there and have a word with Saul? I tried to warn him off before, but it didn't do any good. He might listen to you.'

'And pigs might fly. No, this is a job for a man.'

'He's a lot younger than Dad,' Alice told her. 'If it came to a dust-up I'm afraid Dad would get hurt.'

'Then my Joe can go as well,' her aunt said decisively. 'This can't go on, Alice. Surely you can see that?'

Alice *could* see it, and looking at the three grim faces around her, she knew that there was going to be big trouble ahead.

★   ★   ★

Meanwhile, the subject of their debate was giving some serious thought to Saul's proposition.

She loved him, and the thought of never seeing him again was too much for her.

The idea of never seeing her parents again also caused her a momentary pang, but that was life, wasn't it? Women got married and went to live with their husbands. The Bible said that was what you were supposed to do. She would go with Saul.

Mum and Dad mightn't like it at first, but once she was married they would soon welcome her back, especially after the grandchildren came along.

In the meantime there was a big hurdle to overcome; how to get out of the house despite their protests. Well, that, too, was easily solved. She disliked the idea of leaving without saying goodbye but it had to be done. Saul meant to travel on the night train, so all she had to do was retire to bed as usual and then slip out of the house when the household was asleep. She would leave a note, of course; that was only right.

Now the decision had been made she began to feel excited. She couldn't possibly go on working in such a state, so she went to Mrs Grier, putting on a sick face as she went.

'I'm not feeling very well, Mrs Grier.'

'What's the matter with you?' her employer said suspiciously.

'I don't know. I feel so hot but I keep shivering,' Vicky improvised. 'I'm sorry, Mrs Grier . . .'

'All right, all right, let's have less of the song and dance. You can't go in the water in that state, so you'd best get off home.' Mrs Grier spoke in her usual impatient tone. 'You'd better be recovered by morning, though, or you needn't bother coming back at all. I need someone I can rely on, not a sickly girl who's away more than she's here.'

This wasn't strictly fair as, by and large, Vicky had worked well. Still, she was used to Mrs Grier's grumbles and usually ignored them. She made no reply, but hurried into the hut to change. She had to get home to prepare for her departure — and her new life!

★ ★ ★

'Bit of excitement in there,' Ida told Minnie, who had come struggling into the kitchen with a pail of dirty water and a scrubbing brush.

'What's going on, then? Bertie lost his job, has he?'

'No — it's that Vicky from next door. She's playing fast and loose with the Punch and Judy man and Madam says as how it's got to be put a stop to before things goes too far.'

'Cor! We see some life in this house, don't we? I tell you something else that's maybe going too far, Ida. That bloke what's staying next door — Mr Monty something — he's been walking out with that Miss Carrington from down the way.'

'Oh, everybody knows that. You're

behind the times, Minnie, you are.'

'That's all you know. You remember how Madam sent me up to speak to the butcher, to chivvy him up 'cos he never sent them lamb chops she ordered? Well, I stood behind Miss Carrington and another lady and I heard them talking.'

'Minnie! You know what Matron always said! Listeners never hear any good of themselves.'

'Matron don't know nothing. They wasn't talking about me anyway. The other lady — the one I don't know — she says, 'How are you getting along with your young man, then?' and Miss Carrington says, 'Very well, thank you. I don't think it will be long before he takes me to meet his mother.' And we all know what that means, don't we, Ida?'

'Yes,' Ida breathed. 'Fast work, I call it. He's hardly been here a fortnight, and she's set her cap at him already. I can't say as I blame her. Miss Alice told Master Bertie that he has a picture at his bedside of a big fancy house. That's their family home, that is. Some people have all the luck.'

They turned around as they heard the front door slam. Ida ran to see what was going on and was all agog when she came back. 'They've gone next door, Min. Madam, and Bertie, and Miss Alice. Now the fat's in the fire and no mistake! That Miss Vicky's going to get a telling off she won't forget when her dad finds out what she's been up to!'

Uproar at Stella Maris

Glancing out of an upstairs window, Florence groaned. Old Mr Barker had been hovering near the front door and was now accosting her husband as he arrived home from work. He obviously intended to speak to Alf as he'd threatened, which would really set the cat among the pigeons.

The two men stayed on the front steps for several minutes and then came into the house. Florence tiptoed on to the landing from where she tried to peer over the banisters without being observed from below. She was amazed to see them entering the parlour together. The door closed with a snap.

This in itself was unusual. It was an unwritten law that the family stayed out of the parlour when there were guests in the house; Alf and Florence had comfortable chairs in the kitchen while the girls had their own rooms to relax in. Furthermore, Alf left 'that side of things' to his wife, meaning that he was quite happy for her to run her little summer business as long as he didn't have to be involved. Now he had shut himself in the parlour with one of the guests — and what a guest!

She came down the stairs, still treading lightly, and put her ear to the parlour door. Regrettably it was made of solid oak and very little sound filtered through. She could hear the hum of voices but could not make out what was being said. Frustrated, she gave up and went out to the kitchen. At least they weren't shouting at each other, which was a good thing.

At that moment, the back door burst open and her sister marched in, followed by an excited Bertie and a shame-faced Alice.

'We have to talk to you, Flo!' Edie began.

'Not now, Edie. We're in the middle of something here,' Florence replied, distracted and worried.

'Such as what? It doesn't look like it to me!'

'Alf's in the parlour with Mr Barker!' Florence hissed.

Understanding dawned on Edie's face. 'Oh! Are they talking about you-know-what?'

'How do I know? He was lying in wait for Alf when he got back from work and they came in together. So far war hasn't broken out, but I'm expecting to hear something any minute now!'

Bertie and Alice exchanged bewildered glances. They both knew that Mr Barker was a very demanding man — why else would he have moved from Sea View to Stella Maris — but why should he complain to Alf about whatever it was, and not Florence?

'I'm sorry, Edie,' Florence went on, 'but you can see how I'm placed. Unless you can explain what you've come for in words of one syllable, it'll have to wait.'

'Yes, yes, I see. I'll come back later, then.'

'But Mum!' Bertie protested. 'You said . . . '

'Never mind what I said, our Bertie.' His mother took him by the shoulder and pushed him towards the door. Poor Florence, she thought — never mind what was going on between the two men, there would be a different sort of row when Florence learned about Vicky's silly goings on.

Alice took another look at her mother's set face and glided to the inner door. Whatever was going on, she wanted no part of it. She recognised storm clouds when she saw them.

At long last the parlour door opened and Alf emerged, looking perplexed.

'Get us a cuppa, love,' he said. 'I'm that parched I could drink a gallon.'

'Not until you tell me what's been going on in here, Alf Williams!' Florence retorted.

'Wouldn't you like to know!' He grinned and his wife relaxed. If he was able to joke about it, things couldn't be too bad.

'Alf! For goodness sake, spit it out!'

'I'm too dry to spit, gal!' Alf insisted. 'Just get me that tea and then I'll tell you all about it.'

When they were sitting at the table with their tea, with Florence wishing she had something stronger to calm her down, he began at last.

'You'll never guess what the old boy wanted.'

'What?' Florence resisted the urge to brain him with the teapot, but an unconscious Alf was no good to her at this stage of the game.

'He only wants to buy this house!'

'Buy the house? Whatever for?'

'To live in, of course. He's just retired and he's fed up with city life. He's always wanted to live near the sea, the 'bracing ozone' as he calls it, and he reckons that Stella Maris is just his cup of tea. Speaking of which, is there any more in that pot?'

Florence refilled his cup. 'But why

here? This house isn't for sale. I hope you told him that! If he must live in Caxton, let him find somewhere else.'

'Ah, but that's not all. He wants you and all!'

Florence swallowed hard. 'Me?' she squeaked.

'Yes. It seems he favours your cooking, and he's quite impressed by the service here. One up to you, love! He says he's prepared to keep you on as cook-general after we've sold the place to him, and I can stay as general dog's-body.'

Florence didn't know whether to laugh or cry. So much for being a kept woman!

'But why go the length of buying the place, if that's what he wants? It surely can't be because I'm not prepared to take on permanent boarders. There are plenty of landladies willing to do that.'

'He doesn't want to be a boarder in someone else's home. That's too vulgar for the old boy. No, he can afford to have his own establishment, and he thinks that Stella Maris is just the ticket.'

'Well, blow me down with a feather!'

'That's the way I felt at first, love, but let's not dismiss it out of hand. It could be just what the doctor ordered.' Alf took a swig of his tea and continued, his eyes alight with excitement. 'We'd get a good price for this place, or we won't sell. Then we'll have a nice little nest egg for our old age. You'll have less work to do, with just one old gent to look after instead of people coming and going all the time. I know he can be a bit difficult . . . '

'Difficult!' Florence interrupted.

'But better the devil you know than one you don't,' Alf persisted. 'I mean to say, all the people we've had so far have been decent enough, but it's only a matter of time before we get someone who'll walk off with the teaspoons, isn't it? Any road, I told the old boy we'd give this some thought.'

'I don't need to give it some thought!' Flo slapped her hand firmly down on the chenille tablecloth. 'First of all, this is my house! Aunt Clara left it to me and what I say goes! I like the work I'm doing, meeting new people and striving to meet high standards here. When I do something right they tell me so, and that makes me feel good. I've spent all these years looking after you lot, with never a word of praise from one of you. Can't you see how that makes me feel?'

'But that's a wife's job, love — looking after a husband and kiddies.'

'I know, Alf, I know.' she looked at him rather sadly. He'd never understand, not in a million years. 'But if we do what Mr Barker wants, it would be nothing more or less than going into service. I've never been in service, Alf, and I don't want to start at my time of life.'

'Nothing wrong with being in service, love.' He was still bewildered. 'Both my sisters were in service before they married, and proud to be doing good work, they were.'

'I never said there was. Service is all right for those with no other choice, but don't you see, this house has given us a step up? We're property owners now, able to come and go as we please. It's not everybody can say that.'

'Come and go as you please? When did you last get a day off? Those little orphans next door get more time to themselves than you do.'

'That's not the point, Alf. I'm my own boss now, and that means a lot to me. And think about this. Say we sell to Mr Barker and agree to be his servants. What if he gets fed up with us and turns us out? Or what if he dies? He's not a young man any more. Then what?'

'Then we take our money and start up somewhere else. We can't lose. In fact, we should do better because Mr Barker will be paying us a wage all the time we're here.'

They were going round in circles and Florence sighed.

'Look, this is getting us nowhere, and

I have to cook tea. Let me think about this for a bit and we can make up our minds later.'

Her mind was already firmly made up but Florence had been married for a long time and had learned that the best way to handle Alf was to let him think he had the upper hand.

Meanwhile she should be able to come up with some convincing reason for leaving things as they were.

She didn't feel at all sorry for Mr Barker. He might be disappointed but they owed him nothing. He would be able to find another house and servants easily enough. It was too bad that he and Edie didn't get on since she was thinking of selling up. If he bought Sea View instead, she could still stay next door to Florence and they would all be pleased.

As she lit the gas under the potatoes Florence wondered if it was worth asking Edie if she might consider it. All that fuss about wanting different rooms and special menus would be fair enough if he actually owned the house rather than being one of a number of guests, and Edie might not mind when she had nobody else to cater to. Yes, the idea might well appeal to her, if it was put to her in the right way.

★　★　★

Vicky managed to pull the wool over her mother's eyes quite nicely. It helped that Florence's thoughts seemed to be elsewhere when she sidled in through the back door. Florence absently accepted her explanation that she'd been sent home early because she was unwell, and although surprised that her mother failed to fuss over her as usual, Vicky was grateful for the reprieve. She ran upstairs and shut her bedroom door tightly.

Vicky hugged her secret to herself. This time next week she would probably be Mrs Higgins, she fantasised. She had only a vague idea as to what was involved in getting married.

There wouldn't be a church ceremony, of course, because you had to have the banns called three weeks in a row, she knew that much. But you could have a civil ceremony. She didn't know how you went about arranging that, but Saul would be able to find out, she was sure.

She began to sing and then stopped abruptly, remembering she was supposed to be ill. Once everyone was safely tucked up in bed, she could make her move.

She had no compunction about leaving Caxton-on-Sea behind. She hadn't been here long enough to put down roots. Leaving Leamington had been a wrench and she hadn't been in touch with her old school friends since, but she'd got over that. It was amazing how love made you see everything in a different light.

In her mind she sheered away from any thought of how Dad would react. He wouldn't be pleased, that she knew, but he would come round in time. He was her father, after all! She wondered what Saul's parents were like, and if she'd be taken to meet them soon. He hadn't mentioned them, but perhaps that was because they were back in Ireland.

She opened her suitcase, wondering how much she could cram into it. The weather was hot just now but she'd need her winter clothes in due course. Could she count on Mum to send them on? Buying all new things might not be possible — she didn't know how much money they'd have. Saul only had his Punch and Judy show to depend on, and that was a seasonal thing.

She picked up a family picture, taken last Christmas in Leamington. They had all gone to a studio which had been set up at Marshall's as a way of bringing people in over the holiday season. Dad was looking self conscious, Mum was beaming, and she and Alice were trying to look nonchalant. That had been before there was any thought of them all moving to Caxton. Vicky cringed at the thought that if Aunt

Clara hadn't left her houses to Mum and Auntie Edie, she would never have met Saul; never have known he existed. Or perhaps they would have met in some other way, for she knew that he was her destiny.

⋆ ⋆ ⋆

On the other side of the bedroom wall Alice was hunched in her armchair, fretting over what lay ahead when Vicky's deception was brought to light. She herself would be in trouble from all sides. She could just hear Dad now: 'It's your responsibility to look after your little sister, Alice. You have failed utterly in your duty to this family.'

Mum would say, 'You should have come to me at once. As soon as you realised your sister was getting herself into difficulty you should have spoken up, no matter what the cost to yourself. I'm so disappointed in you.'

She wriggled her toes in her fluffy bedroom slippers. Why should she get the blame for everything, just because she was the elder of the two sisters? It might have been different when they were small, but Vicky was grown up now — or liked to think she was. Surely the onus should be on her to behave properly?

Her parents wouldn't be the only ones expressing their dismay. Just wait until Vicky felt the weight of their wrath! An avenging angel would have nothing on her when she swooped down on Alice to blame her for 'sneaking' to Mum and Dad! And that wasn't fair because she had kept her anxieties to herself all this time. It was Bertie who'd spilled the beans to Auntie Edie that had brought matters to a head.

Restlessly, Alice went downstairs, where she was greeted by her mother.

'Mum, are you going round to see Auntie Edie this evening?'

'Whatever for?'

'Well, she may be waiting for you. She did come round earlier and she said it was very important.'

'It's probably something and nothing. I'll pop round in the morning. I've a lot on my mind at the moment and I'm in no mood to listen to Edie grumbling about her guests. She doesn't know when she's well off, and her with two little maids to run about after her. Two, I ask you!'

Alice could see how irritated her mother was becoming, and she was afraid to make matters worse. She hurried out of the kitchen, biting her lip.

★   ★   ★

Night came and still Vicky hadn't put in an appearance. Florence had spent an annoying evening during which she'd been unable to settle to anything. It had been one thing after another, with guests appearing to ask silly questions, and Mr Barker asking Alf if they had made up their minds yet about his grand plan.

'Coming to bed, love?' Alf asked,

when all was quiet at last.

'I suppose I may as well, but I know I won't be able to nod off; I'm too keyed up.'

'You'll be resting your weary bones even if you don't fall asleep. Come on, up the apples and pears!'

Lying awake in her room, Alice heard her parents come upstairs. Water ran in the bathroom, doors opened and closed, and at last there was silence.

She strained her ears to hear what Vicky was doing but all was quiet. She must be asleep by now.

Alice heaved a sigh of relief. Things were sure to look different in the morning. She rolled on to her side and was soon dead to the world.

Vicky waited until the house seemed to be asleep. At last she could wait no longer, and she gathered up her possessions and tiptoed down the stairs, carefully avoiding the step which always creaked.

Her heart hammered against her ribs. This was it! She was on her way!

Next door at Sea View, Bertie was unable to sleep. The business with Vicky was preying on his mind. The evening had passed very slowly and still Auntie Flo hadn't called in to see what was so urgent.

'Shouldn't we go over there again?' he'd fretted, but his mother had shaken her head, tight-lipped.

'No, son. Flo knows where I am if she wants to talk to me.'

'But, Mum . . . '

His father had spoken up then. 'Do settle down, Bertie! You're like an old woman, worrying over that girl. I agree she's a bit flighty, but what girl of her age isn't? Leave her alone and she'll come to her senses in time.'

'Alice wasn't,' he protested. 'Flighty, I mean.'

'Well, no. Your cousin Alice was born staid, I reckon, but there, we're all different.'

Bertie persisted like a terrier worrying

at a bone. 'Don't you think we should do something, Mum?'

Edie laughed. 'We all know you're sweet on Vicky, love, but take it from me, no girl wants a young man interfering in her life. You'd get further with her if you ignored her completely. That's what girls are like. Take it from me, I know!'

Red-faced, Bertie slouched away. He couldn't imagine his plump, rosy-cheeked mother as a girl, although he knew she must have been one once. He tried to put Vicky out of his mind and get to work on his model aircraft instead, but he couldn't concentrate and the biplane ended up with a decidedly lop-sided look about it. He muttered a curse and flung the materials down on his desk.

It was the same thing when he went to bed. In his mind's eye, he could still see his Vicky in the arms of that gypsy chap, hugging and kissing in full view of the beach.

He went to the window where he

stood for a while taking in great breaths of salty air. He loved his room. It had been given to him because it was a tiny space, tucked under the eaves, which made it unsuitable for guests, but the lattice window afforded a fine view of the beach and in the daytime he could see everything that was going on there. The families, paddling in the sea or making sand-castles; the donkey stand where he worked; even the hated Punch and Judy tent in the far distance. He knew instinctively that by now that tent would have been packed up and be gone. What he'd seen on the beach had the air of a farewell embrace.

Throwing the window wide he craned his neck to get a look at Stella Maris. All was dark there. He knew which was Vicky's room, but no light showed there either. Down below, a slight movement caught his eye. Was that a figure hovering on the doorstep? A cloud passed over the moon and he was able to see more clearly. Whoever it was had started to run, swinging a suitcase behind her.

Her! He realised then that the figure was female; he could tell by the way she ran — and who would be running out of Stella Maris late at night, carrying a case? Certainly not Auntie Flo. It wouldn't be Alice. So it must be Vicky, running away from home, to join that beastly Punch and Judy man!

Hauling on his dressing-gown he shot downstairs and out into the street, but by the time he got there she had gone. He looked this way and that but there was no sign of her. At that moment, an old proverb came into his head — *He who hesitates is lost*. He was the only one who knew that Vicky was gone, and it was up to him to save her!

He pounded on the front door of Stella Maris until a window opened above and Uncle Alf peered out. 'What the dickens is going on down there? You'll rouse the whole street!'

'It's me, Uncle! Come quick! There's awful trouble!'

Alf withdrew his head and a moment

later the door was flung open and Bertie fell inside. He just had time to register that Auntie Flo was standing beside her husband, a sight to behold with her hair tied up in curling rags, before his uncle had him by the arm.

'Now, then, boy! What do you mean by coming round here at this hour, in your bare feet?'

'What's wrong?' Florence quavered. 'Is it our Edie? Is she sick?'

'It's your Vicky, Auntie. She's run away!'

'Don't be stupid, boy!' Alf roared. 'She's in her bed, fast asleep, same as we was until you come knocking!'

'No, Dad, she isn't. And there's this,' Alice put in.

On hearing the noise, Alice had run at once to her sister's room. She had found an envelope on the mantelpiece, addressed *'To Mum and Dad'*, which no doubt explained everything — or at least as much as Vicky was prepared to tell.

'Read it! Quick!' her father commanded.

'I have gone to be with Saul. I love him and we are going to be married so don't try to stop us. Love, Vicky,' Alice read aloud.

'Who the dickens is Saul?' Alf growled.

'The Punch and Judy man. We tried to tell you, Auntie, but you wouldn't listen. Mum was expecting you all evening, but you never came round. It's not my fault. It isn't, it isn't!'

'All right, our Bertie, just calm down. Nobody's blaming you,' Florence told him. 'You'll have to go after her, Alf. She can't have got far.'

'I'll get dressed,' Alf said, already halfway up the stairs. 'You'd better come with me, lad. Go home and get your clothes on and meet me back here as soon as possible.'

Bertie dashed home and threw on a shirt and a pair of trousers. In spite of his worry, he felt a thrill of excitement. This was better than one of those stories he loved to read in the *Boys' Own Paper!*

'Off we go, then!' his uncle said, when they met in front of Stella Maris five minutes later.

'Where are we going, Uncle?'

'Railway station. She's probably planning to catch the night train out of Caxton.'

'But how do you know, Uncle? What if she isn't? What shall we do then?'

'Use your loaf, boy! What other way is there at this time of night? Do you think they'll be galloping off on one of your donkeys?'

They made their way to the station as fast as they could, but when they pushed their way past the barrier and pounded on to the platform, it was to see the back of the guard's van as the train disappeared round the bend. They were too late!

Alf panted up to a uniformed man who was preparing to lock up the station before going off duty. He looked at the pair in surprise.

'Hello, Alf. What's up? If you've come to meet the train, nobody got off here, and as you well know, there isn't another one until the milk train comes through in the morning.'

'But did anyone get on?' Alf insisted.

'Why, yes, a young couple with a load of stuff they wanted put in the guard's van, and a right old trouble it was, getting it all stowed away. Canvas and boards and that.'

'Never mind that. What about the girl? What did she look like?'

The description the man gave them fitted Vicky.

'That's my girl,' Alf said through gritted teeth. 'The silly fool is eloping with that blasted fellow from the beach!'

'What do we do now, Uncle?'

'I'll tell you what we'll do. That train stops at Leeminster while they take on water, isn't that so, Ben?'

'Yes, yes.'

'Then you just open up again and we'll telegraph to Leeminster and tell them to hold the couple there. Call out the constables as well. We won't let that fellow get away with this!'

'But how will we get there?' Bertie chimed in. 'There isn't another train before morning!'

'We'll get your dad out of bed and he can harness up that old cab horse of his. Your legs are younger than mine, lad, so you run home and get Joe started. I'll go on to the stable and wait for you there. Run, boy!'

So Bertie sped off, hoping to be allowed to go with the men to Leeminster. He, Bertie, was Vicky's faithful knight, even if he wasn't galloping to her rescue on a fine white horse, but sitting behind an elderly hackney. He couldn't wait to see her face when they burst into the station waiting-room where the police would be holding them. She'd be furious, of course, but in time she'd come to realise it was all for the best, and she'd be grateful then.

★   ★   ★

'You took your time!' Saul grumbled when Vicky panted into the station. 'I thought you weren't coming. Have you got your ticket?'

'Well, no. Didn't you buy one for me?'

'The ticket office isn't open at this time of night. I had to come earlier in the day and get mine then.'

She pouted. 'You could have bought mine as well.'

'Waste of money if you hadn't turned up.' He shrugged.

'Then what am I going to do? What if they put me off the train when they see I haven't paid?'

'You don't know much, do you? This isn't a corridor train. There won't be anyone to make you do anything. You can pay at the other end if you want to be a good little girl, though there's ways of dodging the ticket collector if you put your mind to it.'

This made Vicky feel slightly uncomfortable, but when the train pulled in she followed Saul meekly on board into an empty carriage. He made no effort to help her lift her case up on the luggage rack and it was so heavy that it gave her quite a struggle.

Her heart was in her mouth until she heard the whistle blow, and the train moved off, travelling slowly until it cleared the station and then picking up speed. She had expected to see her parents arriving at any moment but now they were actually under way, with no hitches, she was able to breathe a sigh of relief.

Now that her great adventure had actually started it all seemed too good to be true. Saul seemed rather grumpy but it was late at night and he was probably tired. As for herself, she was tingling with excitement and wanted to talk.

'You bring anything to eat?' he demanded.

'Um, no. I didn't have a chance.'

'You live in a guest house, don't you? Your Ma must have a pantry full of food. You could have nicked something on the way out.'

'Well, I didn't,' she told him, and the pair lapsed into a sulky silence.

Vicky leaned back in her seat, feeling resentful. As if the previous few hours hadn't been quite nerve-racking enough without going into the pantry and knocking over the pots and pans.

'I've brought my birth certificate,' she began.

'Oh, yes?' He didn't seem interested; perhaps he didn't realise the significance of this.

'I expect we'll have to produce it when we go to get the marriage licence, won't we? I hope you've got yours.'

He sat up. 'Marriage licence? Who said anything about marriage?'

'But I thought . . . '

'To hell with what you thought! Women are all the same! Just let a man show a bit of interest and they've got a ring through his nose and half a dozen brats needing to be fed. Well, that's not for me!'

Vicky gasped with shock and hot

tears sprang to her eyes. She couldn't understand what was happening. She had given up everything for him — and now this! If he'd changed his mind he should have said so before she got on the train with him. Then she could have crept back home before she was missed. She said as much, and he threw back his head and laughed.

'I've not changed my mind, Mavourneen! You're a dear little thing and we can have a lot of fun together, if only you'll take that look off your face. It's enough to sour the milk, so it is.'

'But we can't live together without being married, Saul,' she protested. 'It wouldn't be right.'

He shrugged and something told her that no amount of pleading would make him change his mind. She wondered what she could do now. She had a bit of money saved up, the proceeds of her short-lived job, but that wouldn't last long. She would have to decide between doing as Saul expected, or trying to get some sort of job to support herself

— she would never be able to face them all if she went back home.

Her thoughts were interrupted when the train slowed to a halt.

'Where are we?' Saul demanded.

Vicky peered out the window. 'The sign says Leeminster,' she told him.

'Are there many people waiting to get on? I hope nobody wants to get in here. I'd like us to have a bit of privacy on the journey.' He smiled winningly but Vicky didn't notice. She was too busy scanning the platform.

'There's two policemen. They're just standing there — it doesn't look like they mean to get on. I expect they're just waiting for something.'

'What? Where? Let me see!' Saul pushed her aside roughly.

He looked wildly up and down, then suddenly moved to the other side of the carriage and wrenched open the opposite door.

'Saul, what are you doing?' Vicky shrieked. 'You'll fall! The platform's on this side!'

But Saul jumped even as she tried to pull him back. Moments later, he could be seen scrambling up the bank and as she watched, helpless, he disappeared from view.

The other door opened behind her and a helmeted head poked inside. 'Miss Vicky Williams? I must ask you to come with me, please.'

She sank back in her seat, all the breath knocked out of her. Her bid for freedom and romance had failed miserably.

★　★　★

She soon found herself seated on a hard station bench with a sturdy constable on either side. The younger one seemed sympathetic, and seemed inclined to put her at ease.

'Sorry we can't get you a cup of tea, miss,' he told her, 'but as you see, the station is closed at this time of night. I could get you a bar of chocolate from the slot machine, though, if you're hungry?'

'No, thank you,' she whispered, past the lump in her throat. 'I couldn't eat anything.'

'I don't doubt your pa will have you on bread and water for a month,' the older constable said with some relish. He had daughters of Vicky's age and if ever they tried a trick like this, he would give them what for and no mistake!

'What's going to happen to me now?' she sniffed, raising a woebegone face to look at him.

'Your pa is on his way, miss. What happens then is up to him.'

'I won't have to go to court or anything, will I?'

'Not unless they charge you with trying to defraud the railway,' he replied, having already seen that she was travelling without a ticket. It was unlikely that they would, of course, but he wanted to give her a bit of a fright. She was just a silly young thing and hadn't gone too far down the wrong road as yet.

'We weren't doing anything wrong,'

she snivelled. 'I thought we were going to be married, I really did.'

The constable had heard it all before.

'I know his type,' he said firmly. 'First they get all lovey-dovey and make some poor girl fall for them, hook, line and sinker. Then when she's ruined and disgraced, it's off to London and no turning back.'

The clip clop of approaching hooves broke the silence.

'That'll be your pa now, miss.'

Vicky shrank back. 'No, please, I don't want to see him!'

'It's either that or we take you back with us and you spend a night in the cells!'

'Where is he? Let me at him!' Alf burst on to the platform, swinging his fists as he came. Uncle Joe was right behind him.

'He's made his escape, sir, I'm sorry to say. But here's your girl, safe and sound, so all's well that ends well.'

'You blithering idiot, Vicky!' Alf roared. 'Just wait till I get you home! I'll teach you to go running off with the first man who whispers sweet nothings in your ear! And when I'm finished with you I'll hand you over to your mother, and she'll have a thing or two to say as well!'

Vicky recovered a little of her old defiant spirit as she stood up to face her father. 'You don't know what it's like to be young and in love!' she snapped. But truth to tell, something had died inside her now that Saul had shown his true colours.

'We'll see about that,' Alf grunted, propelling her towards the waiting cab. She stopped short when she caught sight of Bertie, who was waiting with the horses.

'Traitor!' she hissed.

Vicky to the Rescue

Life at Stella Maris settled down after the events which had electrified them all earlier in the week. Vicky was confined to her room until further notice with her meals brought to her on a tray. It was supposed to be a punishment but she was glad to stay there with only her novels for comfort; she was too ashamed to face anyone. Alice felt sorry for her sister and managed to smuggle in some new library books.

Mr Barker sought out Alf and told him that he'd changed his mind about buying the house and taking Florence on as his cook. He'd been passing through the hall on his way to breakfast when Vicky had been brought in, struggling and sobbing, and although Florence had given some lame excuse for the state the girl was in, it was obvious that something was very wrong.

Obviously this was not a well regulated household!

'I thought he might come to you instead and try to buy Sea View,' Florence said to Edie later, when she was telling her sister all about Vicky's escapade.

'Not on your life! I'd have sent him off with a flea in his ear if he had!'

'He had quite a shock when he found we weren't quite the thing,' Florence sighed. 'He probably thinks you're tarred with the same brush, being my sister.'

'Never mind about him, silly old buffer. We're well rid of him. What's more important, how are things with Vicky? I wish they'd caught that chap — he deserves a good thrashing for enticing her away like he did.'

Florence shook her head. 'I'm glad he did make a dash for it, or I'm afraid Alf might have killed him. Then they'd have hanged him for murder.'

'Surely not. Any judge would under-stand if a father took matters into his own hands in a case like this.'

'He might understand, all right, but the law is the law.'

Edie patted her sister on the hand. 'Well, it didn't happen, so that's one less thing for you to worry about. What's going to happen to Vicky now?'

Florence pulled a face. 'Knowing my Alf as I do, it'll be many a long day before she goes anywhere unchaperoned. Which reminds me, I want your Bertie to take a note to Mrs Grier tomorrow. I shall explain that she isn't well, and won't be able to go in the water again this summer.

'You know what Alf thinks,' she continued. 'He thinks that Higgins must be a wrong 'un, quite apart from persuading Vicky to run off with him. Why else would he have made a dash for it as soon as he saw the bobbies? He couldn't have known that we'd set the police on to Vicky the way we did.'

'I hope she's not going to hold this against our Bertie for the rest of his life,' Edie fussed. 'He acted for the best, and let's face it, if it wasn't for him she'd be long gone, and perhaps you'd have never heard from her again.'

'She'll have to get over it — that's all there is to it.'

★ ★ ★

As it happened, Bertie no longer cared. He was beginning to find that Ida was much more his style. She was full of tales about life in the orphanage, and always managed to put in a bit of extra zip when she told the stories, making them sound more interesting than they probably were.

Not only that, she never snubbed Bertie as Vicky had always done, and she took an interest in his model planes and didn't scoff when he mentioned that some day ordinary people might fly from one place to another, instead of always taking the train.

'Right now it's just a few pilots,' he explained, 'but some day, who knows what might happen?'

He told her about the two American brothers, Orville and Wilbur Wright, who had invented a flying machine just four years earlier. Other people had tried using gliders, but they were the first to travel in a mechanical aircraft.

He had gleaned this knowledge from articles in the *Boys' Own Paper*, but she wasn't aware of that and listened to his speeches with great respect.

'Would you like to come to the Bioscope with me some evening?' Bertie asked suddenly, greatly daring.

'Oo, yes, please!' she gasped. 'But won't your Mum mind?'

'I don't care if she does!' he said stoutly. Stella Maris was not the only household where a revolution was going on!

★   ★   ★

In her lonely room, Vicky tried to puzzle out what had happened. She felt very resentful towards her parents, who had placed her in this position. She was convinced that if the policemen hadn't appeared on the platform at Leeminster, everything would have worked out all right in the end.

Although taken aback by Saul's attitude towards marriage, she was confident that he would have changed his mind in due course. Once they'd been well away from Caxton-on-Sea he would have been his old, loving self.

When nobody was about she left her room and went to gaze out of the landing window, which had a good view of the sands. She fantasised that if she stared long enough the striped tent of the Punch and Judy show would appear there. Then she would run down the promenade and along the beach, and hurl herself into Saul's arms.

Then a thought struck her. Perhaps it wasn't over yet! When the hue and cry died down, he might come back to claim her, or perhaps he might write to her in care of Mrs Grier.

She knew Alice would pour cold water on these dreams if she confided in her, but then Alice had never been in love — and despite all that had happened, Vicky was still very much in love with Saul Higgins.

* * *

Vicky wasn't the only young woman to be experiencing the pangs of unrequited love. Alice happened to be in the front hall of Stella Maris when the doorbell rang, and she opened up to find a smartly-dressed young lady smiling at her. She recognised the visitor as Miss Mona Carrington from Mon Repos.

'Good day, Miss Williams. I'd like to speak to Mr Montague-Hayes, please. Could you let him know I'm here?'

'Oh, I'm so sorry, Miss Carrington, but Monty — Mr Montague-Hayes, that is — left two days ago.'

Mona's hand flew to her mouth. 'Oh, dear. How odd that he didn't tell me. Where was he going, do you know? Was he on his way home to his mother, I wonder?'

Not another one! Alice thought. Men really are the limit!

She hesitated, wondering what to do for the best.

'He told us he was going to Paris,' she said at last. Mum would be so cross at her for passing on this information because she was strict about the guests' privacy. If it became known that their personal privacy was being violated by anyone at Stella Maris, they would lose custom.

'Paris!' Mona shrilled, and to Alice's horror she began to cry.

'You'd better come inside, Miss Carrington. I'll make you a cup of tea if you don't mind sitting in the kitchen. We don't serve guests at this time of day.'

Meekly Mona followed her in and was soon toying with an oatmeal biscuit which she reduced to crumbs on her plate.

'Why Paris?' she asked. 'Monty told me his father didn't want him to have the Grand Tour like his friends were getting. He sounds a bit mean, to me, don't you think so? Perhaps Monty has done especially well in his university examinations, and his father changed his mind.'

Privately Alice thought it might have to do with a lack of money. She was sure that Monty was a braggart, and she even wondered now if the grand house shown in his bedside photo belonged to his family at all!

'I've been expecting an invitation to go to Monty's home and meet his mother,' Mona said, 'but it seems she's not well and can't be disturbed just now.'

This confirmed Alice's suspicions.

'I don't suppose it will hurt if I let you have his home address,' she said. Her mum would be furious, but Alice had learned her lesson and never again would she cover up for someone else's misdeeds. On this occasion she was probably being cruel to be kind.

Miss Carrington left, clutching the

precious piece of paper which would allow her to contact Monty again.

★　★　★

Vicky was still causing everyone a great deal of concern. 'You don't suppose she's going to drown herself, do you?' Alice asked anxiously.

'Of course not!' her mother scolded. 'Not even Vicky would be that silly.'

Alice wished she could feel as sure. Her sister had remained in her room for several days, scarcely eating enough to keep a mouse alive, until Florence had began to worry.

'She's as pale as a ghost, Alf. Do you think we should call the doctor?'

'No need for that, love, but p'raps it's time to get her out into the fresh air. Take her for a walk down the beach every day. That'll put the colour back in her cheeks.'

So Vicky reluctantly went outside, choosing her moment when there were fewer people than usual on the sands.

Although there was little risk of any of the summer visitors knowing about her disgrace, still she didn't feel like exchanging greetings with anyone or giving directions.

On one occasion Mrs Grier walked up to her, asking how she was. Vicky blinked before answering, then realised that Mum had explained that she wasn't well, and that was why she had had to give up her job.

'I'm getting better, thank you,' she managed to say at last.

'That's all right then, but I must say you still look a bit peaky. I expect you're a bit anaemic. Girls your age often are. Eat plenty of liver, that's what you need to do.' Mrs Grier gave her an encouraging pat on the arm and bustled off.

At first Florence insisted that Alice should stay within earshot 'in case', although in case of what she didn't say. The thought hung on the air, unspoken. This particular morning, however, the weather had turned cold and there were few people about. The sea was choppy and since Alice felt the cold at the best of times, Florence had told her to stay at home in the warm.

Vicky walked along the shore alone, her thoughts far away. A man and a woman sat on deck chairs in the lee of the sea wall, huddled in tartan rugs. They were probably staying at one of the other guest houses and had to stay away until tea time, as was the custom. A half-finished sand-castle sagged in front of them, flanked by a brightly-coloured pail filled with sea shells.

A short distance away a small boy, probably their son, was aimlessly kicking a blue ball about. Vicky turned her head away, following the progress of a fishing boat which was slowly chugging its way across the horizon. The mournful cry of the seagulls seemed to echo the cry of her broken heart.

Suddenly she heard a piercing scream from the direction of the two chairs.

The woman was standing up with her hands to her cheeks and her husband was hobbling towards the sea with the aid of two sticks. Vicky hadn't noticed before that he was quite lame. The screams continued as the woman pointed towards the water.

The first thing Vicky saw was the blue ball, bobbing about in the waves, and, not far away from it, she caught a glimpse of a white-covered arm as the little boy went under.

Without stopping to think, she ripped off her shoes and plunged into the sea, frantically heading for the place where she'd last seen the child.

Vicky was not a strong swimmer at the best of times, and she was hampered by her long dress and several petticoats. The boy had been in shallow water, knocked down by an incoming wave because of his small size, and she'd expected to be able to wade out and haul him in. But this was easier said than done. Another wave caught her off balance and down she went, gasping for breath as the water went up her nose.

The boy's father, handicapped as he was, shouted for help at the top of his voice. Vicky hoped there was somebody to take notice. She floundered and was rewarded by the sight of the child, lying in about two feet of water. She reached down and once again was swept off her feet. Somehow she managed to keep her head above water as she felt blindly for the little victim, but the situation was becoming desperate. She feared that when they did get him to shore it might be too late to revive him.

'Please, oh please!' she prayed silently.

Her prayers were answered and this time she was able to grasp the collar of his sailor suit and drag him up the beach.

'I'll take him!' a voice said, and she was more than willing to let the new arrival take over.

She crawled up the beach and lay flat, trying to recover her strength. She must look a terrible sight, she thought, all bedraggled with her dress clinging to her and her hair in rats' tails. The boy's mother wasn't much better, standing by, wringing her hands; she had lost her hat and was moaning piteously.

The father was standing over the young man who had arrived on the scene. Fortunately the newcomer seemed to know what to do, and after what seemed an age the child heaved and spluttered and coughed up water before starting to bawl.

'We can't thank you enough,' the father babbled, glancing from Vicky to the man who had administered artificial respiration to his son. 'As you see, I'm not good for much. I don't know what would have happened if you hadn't gone in after him, miss,' he continued.

'We are deeply grateful,' the mother said, holding the weeping child close to her.

'It's quite all right,' Vicky murmured and the young man smilingly said that he was glad to be of service.

The whole family seemed to have recovered from their fright as they made their way up to the promenade.

'Can I help you up, miss?' her fellow rescuer asked.

'I can manage, thanks.' Vicky scrambled to her feet, trying to smooth down her soaking curls. She was a mess, yet the young man was gazing at her with unconcealed admiration.

'That was a very brave thing you did back there,' he told her.

'Oh, it was nothing,' she murmured. 'I used to work at the bathing machines, so I'm used to going in the water. It's a good thing you knew what to do, though. I was afraid he wasn't going to come round.'

'Ah, that was simple enough,' he told her. 'I'm a medical student, you see, in London. I'm here on holiday and I always come out at this time of day, taking my constitutional.'

Vicky smiled. 'And a good thing, too.'

'Shouldn't we introduce ourselves?' he asked, holding out his hand to her. 'I feel as if we already know each other well after sharing an experience like this. My name is Brian Hatcher.'

'I'm Vicky Williams.'

'Are you on holiday, too, Miss Williams?'

'No, no. I live here, with my family. My mother runs a boarding house here. Stella Maris, it's called.'

'I know it. In fact I have to walk right past it to reach the place where I'm staying. May I escort you home? I would suggest that you should waste no time in getting dried off.'

Vicky could hardly refuse, so they walked briskly past the piled-up deck chairs, the abandoned stage where the pierrots performed, and the kiosk which sold buckets and spades, until they reached the promenade, and from there they made their way to her home.

Alice had been keeping watch at the front window, and now she burst out of the door, clucking like a hen. 'Vicky, oh, Vicky! What have you done? Mum, Mum! Come quickly, do! I told you it wasn't safe! Didn't I say?'

'Oh, do hush up, our Alice! Give me a chance and I'll tell you!' Vicky mumbled.

The medical student was clearly puzzled by this exchange, but when Florence arrived at the door he hastened to explain the situation.

'Miss Williams was very brave indeed. She rescued a child from drowning and had just managed to bring him out of the sea when I came on the scene. You'll be glad to hear that the boy is quite all right now.'

Florence took charge at once. 'Upstairs and get those wet things off,' she ordered. 'You run a hot bath for your sister, Alice, and stop behaving like a ninny. As for you, sir, perhaps you'd like a hot cup of tea after all the excitement?'

'Thank you, that would be very nice. I'm Brian Hatcher, by the way, and I take it you are Mrs Williams.' They smiled at each other as he stepped over the door mat.

Gentlemen Callers

Florence turned the letter over in her hand, looking perplexed. 'I don't know what I'm going to do about this,' she remarked to Alice. 'This is for that Monty chap who stayed here recently.'

'Can't you re-address it to his home? We have a record of that in the register.'

'That's the funny thing, gal. It's got a Caxton postmark and it was sent to him there. It's been sent back by a Mrs Montague-Hayes, who must be his mother. It seems odd that she doesn't know her son's whereabouts.'

Alice guessed at once what had happened. 'I wonder if it's a letter from that Miss Carrington, who lives with her aunt at Mon Repos? I understand she was seeing something of Monty while he was here.'

Florence sniffed at the envelope. 'Scented notepaper! Well, it's come from a woman, all right, but how did she know where to send it? I suppose Monty gave it to her.' Fortunately she answered her own question before Alice had to confess to giving out confidential information.

'I want to go to the library, Mum. I can pop in and give the letter to Miss Carrington if you like. That's if she did send it in the first place.'

It was Mona herself who answered the door when Alice called. She put her finger to her lips as she beckoned Alice in.

'Aunt is upstairs lying down. Come into the morning room before you say anything.'

'I'm afraid you're going to be disappointed,' Alice told her, as she handed the letter over. 'This arrived this morning.'

Mona took it with a little cry. 'Oh, dear, I quite thought he'd be home by now, but where on earth can he be? It looks as if his mother doesn't know either, if she thought he was still staying with all of you.' Her expression brightened. 'Do you suppose he's coming back to Caxton after he's seen Paris?'

'I'm sorry, no, I doubt it. His trunk has already gone, you see.'

Mona seemed to sag in her chair and Alice's heart went out to her. 'Is everything all right?' she asked. 'Is there anything I can do?'

'There's nothing anyone can do. Monty was my last hope.'

'Your last hope?'

'I really thought he was interested in me, Alice! Do you mind if I call you by your first name?'

'No,' Alice responded. 'I mean, yes, do.'

'I'm not getting any younger and I'd love to have a home and family of my own. I can't bear the thought of spending the rest of my life at my aunt's beck and call.'

Florence would have pointed out that appearing desperate was no way to attract a man, but Alice was less forthright than her mother so she gently said that perhaps Monty had thought of his association with Mona as just a holiday friendship.

'It's that mother of his, of course,' Mona went on. 'She's a terrible snob. Monty says she frowned on every girl he's ever taken home. They're an old family, you know, and she wants to make sure he chooses someone worthy of him.'

Alice reflected that in all likelihood Monty was every bit as snobbish as his mother was supposed to be, for it was he who had gone away without saying goodbye to Mona. His mother probably didn't even know that the girl existed.

'What do you think I ought to do now?' Mona asked, looking pathetic.

'You could always leave here and get a job,' Alice suggested, remembering all the fun she had had working at Marshall's.

Mona stared at her, horrified. 'But what on earth could I do? I couldn't go into service. Aunt would never allow it.'

'Then be a governess or something. Or go and train as a nurse, or a school-teacher.'

But Mona seemed to find an obstacle for every suggestion and at last Alice became tired of her complaints and stood up to leave, saying she had to get to the library before it closed.

Then and there, Alice made up her mind that she herself would be a bit more positive. There was no husband on the horizon for her either, but she wouldn't allow that to spoil her life, as Mona seemed to be doing. Perhaps when winter came there would be some interesting evening classes on offer. She had rather enjoyed French at school, although she hadn't got very far. An advanced course in that language might be fun, and who knew? It might come in useful in the future. Perhaps one day she could even work in Paris?

★ ★ ★

'There you are!' her mother said when she reached home at last. 'I wondered where you'd got to. Did that letter come from Miss Carrington?'

'Yes, I gave it back to her, Mum.'

'That's all right then. Look, I'm sorry to send you out again, but I need a pound of sausages. Would you mind nipping up to the pork butcher's? Your dad is bringing a work-mate home to tea and the pair of them will be hungry after working all day. Oh, and I want you here to help entertain this chap. Vicky can wait on the guests for once.'

'Yes, Mum.' Alice accepted the purse Florence held out to her. She felt a little puzzled. Why on earth she was needed to entertain some ancient colleague of Dad's was beyond her, but if that was what Mum wanted, she was glad to oblige.

It crossed her mind to wonder why they were having sausages when the guests were being served pork chops; preparing two different menus was a nuisance and not something that Mum often did. Perhaps Dad had requested them because they were the old chap's favourite.

Alice's path took her past a small park on the way and as she came closer she heard music; a brass band was giving a performance in the bandstand there. The lively strains of Johann Strauss's Radetsky March met her ears. It was one of her favourites and she found herself keeping in step with a smile on her face.

By the time she reached the shop she was in good humour. She must come to hear these band concerts more often.

Florence seemed flustered when Alice reached home. 'I thought you were never coming!' She looked her daughter up and down, a critical expression on her face. 'I hope you're going to change before your father gets home!'

'What's wrong with what I've got on?' Alice's blue serge skirt with the bands of braid on the bottom was fairly new, and the white blouse with its leg o' mutton sleeves was clean enough.

'I think you should put a nice frock on, dear. How about your yellow one?'

'The hem's coming down on that.'

'Then get a needle and thread and see to it! How many times have I told you never to put away anything that needs repairing? Get along now, quick march!'

Puzzled, Alice did as she was bid. It was the work of just a few minutes to repair her second-best dress. She hated to admit it but Mum was right — it was just as easy to insert a few stitches as it was to make temporary repairs with a safety pin! However, she still couldn't understand what all the fuss was about.

Nevertheless, she changed out of her skirt and blouse and quickly washed her face and hands.

'They've come!' Vicky hissed, as she passed through the hall on her way to the conservatory, carrying a loaded tray.

Alice, holding up her skirts as she made her way down the stairs so as not to step on the hem again, asked what

Dad's friend was like.

'You're in for a shock!' Vicky replied, pulling a funny face.

'Thanks for warning me!'

What on earth was going on, Alice wondered. There must be something different about the man. Perhaps he was a Boer War veteran, like Uncle Joe, another poor soul who had been badly wounded over there and lost an eye or an arm. Or perhaps he had a rather obvious scar on his face.

Her heart contracted with sympathy. She must be careful not to let any pity show in her eyes, thereby hurting his feelings. She was a kindly girl who would never willingly inflict pain on another person.

'Here's Alice now!' Mum said brightly.

The visitor stood up politely, and as Vicky had warned her, Alice did indeed get a shock.

'This is Jack Fry,' Dad said. 'Jack, this is my daughter, Alice.'

'We've met already,' Jack said,

extending a hand to Alice. He was beaming and she gazed back at him in delight, unable to say anything by way of reply. For a moment she felt that her heart had stopped beating altogether.

So *THIS* was Jack Fry!

'You've already met?' Mum repeated, surprised.

'Yes, Mrs Williams. I went to the Palais de Danse one night and your daughter was kind enough to give me a dance,' the young man explained, his eyes never leaving Alice's face. 'Then she went to join your other daughter, and I lost sight of her. I haven't been able to go there again because of work, but I'm delighted to renew her acquaintance now.'

★ ★ ★

'Pass the potatoes, Alice! Don't keep Mr Fry waiting!'

In a daze, she did as Mum said. She had thought about Jack so much but when he hadn't appeared at the dance hall a second time, she had despaired of ever seeing him again. Vicky had recognised him, of course; that's why she had said Alice would get a shock, but it wasn't a shock, it was a wonderful surprise.

'You didn't tell me you two had met before,' Mum remarked, as she offered a dish of cauliflower to their guest.

'That's because I didn't know who Dad was bringing home,' Alice explained. 'I'd no idea who he was.'

'I'm sure I said it was Jack Fry,' Dad mumbled, spearing a sausage with his fork.

'Maybe you did, but I didn't know who Jack Fry was,' Alice smiled. 'I'd never learned his name. When you said a work-mate I thought it was some elderly chap with a shaggy moustache.'

Jack laughed in delight. 'Well, I hope you're not disappointed, Miss Williams,' he said and her shining eyes gave him his answer.

By the time Mum had served up the jam roly poly pudding, smothered in creamy yellow custard, they were all firm friends. Alice didn't notice when her father raised his eyebrows at his wife, as if to say 'Mission accomplished!'

When the meal was over Alice carried the plates through to the scullery to begin the washing up, but her mother shook her head and made her go back into the kitchen.

'I'm sure you two young things would like to take a walk, wouldn't you? It will help your pudding to slip down.'

'Yes, you get off,' Alf nodded, taking out his pipe.

Alice stole a look at Jack to see how he felt about it, but he rose from the table at once, saying that a walk was just what the doctor ordered.

'I couldn't believe it was you when you came into the room back there,' he told her when they were strolling down the promenade enjoying the evening air. 'Of course, your dad mentioned you and your sister but the name meant nothing to me then.'

'I was surprised as well,' Alice said demurely.

'As I said, I've had to work the night shift since we met, but I meant to come looking for you as soon as I was able. How about you? Have you been back to the Palais since?'

'Once or twice,' Alice admitted.

'And I'm sure you were danced off your feet if you looked as lovely as you do this evening!'

She didn't know how to respond to this so she smiled back, glad that she'd taken trouble with her appearance.

'Now we've found each other again, would you care to come out with me some evening?' Jack asked. 'Perhaps we could go to a concert?'

'That would be nice,' Alice told him. 'There was a good band concert in the park earlier on,' she said. 'They were playing the Radetsky March — it's one of my favourites.'

'Mine, too!' Jack agreed, and they began to exchange views about the type of music they each enjoyed. By the time they returned to Stella Maris, Alice felt as if she'd known Jack all her life. He was good company and easy to talk to.

'I'll send a note home with your dad when I'm free to go out,' he said, as he left her at the door of her house. 'Would that be all right with you?'

Alice agreed that it would. Her parents heard her singing as she raced up the stairs to her room.

'There, I told you it would be all right,' Alf told his wife, a smug expression on his face.

'Only because they already knew each other,' Florence said tartly. 'And we won't go sending out invitations to the wedding yet awhile, Alfred Williams!'

'I wouldn't dream of it, love. But there's no harm in encouraging them a bit, is there?'

'So long as that's all you do,' Florence said in a warning voice. 'Just leave things be now. I'm not having my daughter forced into something she'll live to regret.'

'Nobody's forcing anyone, love. Alice can make up her own mind. All I've done is point her in the right direction. Now, how about another cup of tea?'

★ ★ ★

When the doorbell rang the next evening Florence smiled gleefully at her husband. 'That must be Jack coming back already. That was quick work!'

But it wasn't Jack. It was another young man, taller and with fair hair.

'Good evening, Mrs Williams,' he began.

Florence looked closely at him. 'I've seen you somewhere before, haven't I?' she asked.

'I brought Miss Williams home the day she rescued that little boy from drowning,' he reminded her politely.

'Oh, of course. Do come in! I'm sure my husband would like to meet you!'

'And what can we do for you?' Alf asked pleasantly enough, when Brian Hatcher, as he introduced himself, had explained himself a second time.

'Um, well, I really came to enquire after Miss Williams' health after her experience.'

'Oh, she's as right as rain,' Alf said. 'She's as strong as a horse, is our Vicky.'

'Oh, that's good.'

An awkward silence followed. Alf was determined not to give the young man any encouragement, yet he could hardly show him the door for no good reason.

However, Brian Hatcher was used to standing up to the senior men at his hospital and he knew that if he retreated meekly he might never see Vicky again. He wasn't prepared to let that happen.

'May I speak to Miss Williams and judge for myself how she is? As I explained to her last time we met, I'm a medical student in my last year. I'll be a fully-fledged doctor as soon as I pass my finals. If I can't speak to her today I shan't be able to see her at all, as I return to London tomorrow.'

'I suppose it can't hurt,' Alf decided,

in response to his wife's wild signals from behind Brian's back. 'You fetch her down, Flo. They can sit in the reception room for a bit.'

Intrigued, Vicky hastened downstairs and rather shyly greeted her visitor before sitting on one of the only two upright chairs the small room possessed.

'I'll be in the kitchen if you need me,' Florence said, carefully leaving the door ajar as she left them alone.

'Do you think you're doing the right thing, love?' Alf frowned as she rejoined him. 'After what she got up to recently it'll be a long time before I can bring myself to trust her again.'

'Five minutes in that cubby hole can't lead to much, can it? It might be different if he lived round here; then I'd say we shouldn't encourage it. But he's supposed to be leaving in the morning, and he's not likely to get back here in a hurry, what with having his exams to study for.'

Alf was about to reply to this when

the door was flung open, crashing on to the kitchen wall. 'Here, steady on, you'll have that door off its hinges!'

'Sorry, Dad. There must have been a draught and it got away from me.'

'Where's that young student chap? Has he gone already?'

'No, he's still in Reception. Dad, he wants to know if he can write to me from London.' Vicky blushed.

'And I suppose he wants you to write back!' Florence sniffed.

'Yes, and I — I think I do,' Vicky said hesitantly. 'But I said I'd have to ask you first. Can I? Mum? Dad?'

The light of battle dawned in her father's eyes.

Florence knew that expression and hastened to intervene. 'I don't suppose it can do any harm, can it, Alf?' she pleaded.

Her husband softened at once, all of a sudden seeing not the careworn mother of his grown-up daughters, but the pretty young girl she'd been in their courting days.

'All right, you can do it,' he conceded, 'but with one string attached. You must tell this chap what you did recently, running off into the blue with that rotter from the beach.'

Florence gasped and Vicky turned pale. 'Dad, no!'

But Alf had a set look on his face.

'You can do it that way, or not at all!'

Vicky knew there was no use in arguing. The Rock of Gibraltar was nothing compared to Dad when his mind was made up.

With a look of mute misery at her mother, she left the room.

'What did you want to go and do that for?' Alf glared at his wife. 'Siding with her, after all she's done!'

'Now you listen to me, Alf Williams. I know girls, having been one myself back in the dark ages, and I know our Vicky. She was besotted with that Saul Higgins and it's going to take time for her to get over him. She needs something else to focus on, and writing letters to this nice young man may be just what she needs.'

'Pooh! It was a real eye-opener for her when Higgins rushed off like that, saving his own skin while he left her to face the music. If that hasn't put her right off him, I don't know what would.'

'That's just it,' Florence argued. She had seen her daughter gazing sadly out to sea and knew that love could not be shrugged off so easily. 'If he was to turn up here tomorrow she'd be off with him like a shot, even if she has come to realise he's a bad 'un.'

'That's a lot of eye-wash, Flo! I'd have thought you'd have more sense at your age!'

'Never mind my age! Age has nothing to do with love.' Florence lowered her voice hurriedly, not wanting to be overheard. 'And come to that, what do you mean by telling the poor child she has to confess her sins to this Brian Hatcher?' she hissed. 'You want to humiliate her, is that it?'

'No, of course not! I — '

'And then he'll be horrified and run off just like the other chap. Shame on you, Alf Williams. Well, I'll tell you this much — ' Florence was well into her stride now ' — wanting to protect Vicky does you credit, but you can't keep her close to your side for ever. One of these days she'll be off, whether it's to get wed or something different. And then . . . ' She stopped abruptly as her voice suddenly broke, tears beginning to threaten.

'Steady on, Flo!' Alf came over and put his arm round her shoulders. 'Listen to me for a moment. What I've done is for her own good. It seems to me this Hatcher chap is going places. He'll be a doctor some day soon and that's all to the good.'

Florence nodded, sniffing and searching for a handkerchief.

'Let's say he and our Vicky keep in touch and some day he wants to marry her?' Alf said gently. 'Then somehow it comes out about her elopement. Some gossip tells the story and adds to it, as is always the way.

'By now he has a position to keep up, and he wants a wife as will do him credit. He'd be shocked to learn about Vicky's past and then he'd wash his hands of her. That's twice she's been let down, Flo. Is that what you want for her?'

Florence wiped her eyes viciously. 'No, of course it isn't, but if he's that easily put off he'll spurn her in the next five minutes, so it's as broad as it's long.'

Alf nodded. 'That may be the case, but if it is, better she finds out now before she has time to get ideas about this chap. Better a bit of disappointment now than a broken heart later, see?'

Florence sighed. He was probably right, but she still couldn't help thinking that making Vicky expose her bruised ego to the young medical student was a bit much to expect. She was still only seventeen and had little experience of dealing with some of life's bitter blows.

'Poor child,' she thought. 'She's having to learn a lot the hard way.'

★   ★   ★

Young she might be, but Vicky had great courage when brought to the point. It was this that had enabled her to rush to the young boy's rescue with no thought for her own safety.

She quite liked Brian Hatcher and the idea of exchanging letters with him was inviting. Dad had delivered an ultimatum, so she would just show them all what she was made of.

Clasping her hands tightly together, she wasted no more time. May as well get it over with, she thought.

'My father says I can write to you but I have to tell you something first. Something that may make you want to change your mind.'

'I can't imagine that you could say anything that would have that effect,' he smiled.

'Please, Mr Hatcher . . . '

'Brian!'

'Yes, Brian. Well . . . ' Vicky took a deep breath and haltingly told him the whole sorry tale.

Brian listened quietly.

'And the man? What became of him?' he asked when she paused, her eyes lowered.

'He jumped off the train and ran away,' Vicky said, unable to keep the bitterness out of her voice. 'I haven't seen him since.'

Like the constable at Leeminster Station, Brian Hatcher knew a thing or two about men like Saul Higgins. Not only did he read the London papers, when he could find the time away from his studies, but his work at the hospital had shown him something of the seamier side of life. It wasn't only decent, middle class people or the respectable working poor who were admitted to St Martha's. It also opened its door to what society spoke of as 'unfortunates' or 'fallen women', and he doubted very much if all of them had brought their degradation on themselves.

Sometimes evil men had led them astray by first promising them the moon. At other times so-called gentlemen had preyed upon their female servants, who had been thrown out on the streets to fend for themselves when they had been found to be with child.

Brian's face hardened as he remembered all this and Vicky felt a pain in the pit of her stomach as she noticed this.

'Nothing happened!' she said softly, as a tear ran down her cheek unchecked. 'Please don't look like that, Brian. He did kiss me a few times, but that was all. Please say you believe, me, or I don't think I can bear it.'

Brian's eyes opened wide. 'Of course I believe you, Vicky! If I looked a bit grim for a moment it's only that I was planning what I'd do to Higgins if I ever found him! The man ought to be horse-whipped!'

'That's what Dad said.' Nervousness made Vicky giggle.

'Good! I'm glad we agree on something! Now I'm afraid I must be on my way. I leave early tomorrow and I still have all my packing to do.' He smiled. 'But I'll write as soon as I'm settled back in tomorrow evening.'

Vicky couldn't trust herself to reply.

Florence had been hovering in the hall all this time, listening to the murmur of voices in the little reception room. She searched their faces anxiously as the pair emerged but it seemed that all was well. Vicky looked relieved and the future doctor had a half smile on his face.

'Goodbye for now, Mrs Williams,' he said, holding out his hand. 'May I say goodbye to your husband?'

'He's gone to his allotment, I'm afraid. I'll pass on your message though.'

Florence turned to her daughter when Brian had gone. 'I gather it went all right, you telling him about that other chap?' She still couldn't bring herself to call Saul Higgins by his name.

'I think so, Mum. He seemed to think it wasn't really my fault, and he still wants to write to me. At least, he says he does,' she added doubtfully.

Florence felt like crying. Vicky had always been so trusting and confident, but now it seemed as if she had had all the stuffing knocked out of her.

'If he says he'll write, then he will,' she told her daughter firmly, trying to convince herself as well as Vicky. Blow that Higgins! Now he'd got *her* doubting everyone's good intentions as well!

★ ★ ★

By contrast, Alice's world was becoming brighter by the minute. Jack had called for her three times inside the space of two weeks and she was enjoying his company immensely. Walking along the sea front, or climbing the cliffs to look at the view, was seen in a different light when they were together.

'Where are you from?' she asked him, quite early on. 'I don't think you were born and bred here in Caxton, were you?'

'No, I come from a small place ten miles out.'

'Then what brought you to Caxton? Did you think of going to sea some day?'

'Oh, no, that sort of life doesn't appeal to me. When I was small I wanted to be an engine driver. I suppose most small boys do, but in my case trains have become a lasting love. I had to start off as a railway line maintenance man and now, as you know, I'm a porter, but some day I mean to get taken on as a fireman. If I do well at that I might be able to train as a driver.'

Alice admired him for his ambition. It was good for a man to know where he was going, and what he wanted to be. And increasingly, she began to suspect that when it came to his personal life, he had ideas about that, too — and possibly they included her!

'That's you,' he blurted one night, when he had seen her home and they were saying a sedate goodnight on the doorstep.

Alice looked up to where he was pointing at the name plate over the door. 'I don't know what you mean, Jack.'

'Stella Maris. That means Star of the Sea, doesn't it?'

'Yes, I believe so.' Alice hadn't taken Latin at school, but most people knew what that meant because it was a popular name for houses beside the sea.

'You are my star of the sea,' he said quietly, and Alice was transported to the stars as she received her first kiss from Jack Fry, who was to become the love of her life.

A Rosy Future

September came, and the last of the summer visitors departed. All was quiet at Sea View now and the look of strain which Edie had worn over the past few weeks had gone too. She was able to spend more time with her feet up, enjoying the peace.

The two little maids were able to relax now too.

'No more sweeping up sand from the bedroom floors, thank goodness,' Ida rejoiced.

'And no more being shouted at because some old pudding-face thinks you're too slow,' Minnie put in.

'I hope you're not calling me a pudding-face!' Edie teased, but poor Minnie took her seriously and went pale at the very thought.

'Oh, no, Madam. Never!'

'Don't be silly, Minnie.' Bertie

grinned. 'Mum's only teasing.'

But Minnie wasn't sure and she refused to open her mouth for the rest of the day. Poor Minnie, Edie thought — even after all this time with them, she still seemed scared of her own shadow sometimes.

Edie's husband, Joe, had feared that his job would be gone when the visitors left but his employer had reassured him on that point.

'People still want to come and go by train,' he explained. 'Lots of them stay here year round and of course there's still the hotel. They can't manage without our cabs.'

Bertie's job had come to an end, and he found that he was quite disappointed by this.

'P'raps I'll still be needed?' he had asked hopefully. 'I mean, the donkeys still have to be fed and mucked out and all that.'

'Not unless you want to come with us to the farm,' his boss told him. It turned out that the animals always spent the winter inland.

'If you're still here next summer, lad, come and see me and I'll take you back on for the season. You worked well.' He shook the lad's hand and with that Bertie had to be content.

His mother reckoned that he had grown up a lot over the past summer. He had earned a nice little sum of money, handing over part of it for his keep, and he was more sensible in general and less untidy around the house. Then he'd been the hero of the hour when Vicky had become embroiled with the gypsy chap, although she certainly hadn't appreciated his interference.

There was only one way in which he still showed his immaturity, and that was in making those silly model airplanes. He couldn't wait for the day when he'd get a closer look at the real thing, perhaps even fly in one! It had been four years now since the American inventors had taken a flight in their mechanised flying machine, and according to Bertie that was only the beginning.

'Some day people will be travelling by plane when they come here for holidays,' he promised.

'I do wish you'd stop talking that nonsense,' his mother scolded. 'They won't do any such thing. No sensible folk would ever want to fly.'

'It's the way of the future, Mum,' Bertie insisted. 'It's like these horseless carriages you hear about. Some day everybody will have one, and there'll be no more cabs or carriages.'

'Bang goes your job, then,' she told him. 'No more donkeys on the beach for the kiddies to ride on.'

Bertie took her teasing in good part, which was another sign of his gained maturity.

Edie laughed as she told her husband about Bertie's flights of fancy.

'Leave the boy alone, love. You don't want him growing up too soon.' Joe had something else on his mind. 'Have you made up your accounts since that last lot left? Have we made a profit, or can we expect to see the bailiffs coming in?'

'Oh, we'll have a bit left over when all the bills have been settled up,' she replied, 'but not as much as I'd hoped. It's been an awful lot of work for so little return.'

'Are you still thinking we should sell up and go back to Leamington, then?'

Edie frowned. 'I just don't know what to think. It's been grand owning our own house and Bertie likes it here, I know. Then there's our Flo. She's settled in happily, and she keeps saying she wants to keep me here living next door.'

'I've felt much better in myself since we moved here,' Joe said. 'It's the sea air, I expect. Look, love, I'm earning again, and Bertie will surely be able to get something else now he's got a bit of experience under his belt. I reckon we could manage without you having to take in boarders next year. What do you say?'

Joe saw at once that his wife didn't

look happy at the prospect. 'What's the matter, love?'

When Edie didn't reply, Joe guessed what was on her mind.

'It's them little maids, isn't it? You've got fond of them and you don't want to see them go.'

Was this the time to tell her what he had decided some time back, he wondered? He decided that it was.

'Listen, Edie, love, a shilling a week won't be hard to find, if we're careful. You can keep one of them on to give you a hand in the house. You're not as young as you used to be and you deserve to take things easy.'

Edie shed a little tear at his kindness. Most households, even quite modest ones, kept at least one servant, but that wasn't something the Marsdens had ever dreamed of doing. Before she had inherited Sea View, most of Joe's wages had gone to pay the rent; putting food on the table and clothes on their backs had been a difficult job. Not that it was Joe's fault that he'd been too badly hurt to ever work again at anything which demanded physical strength and endurance.

And here he was, trying to make things easier for her. She looked tenderly at his dear face. He really was one of the best, was Joe.

'If you'd really like to stay on here I'll go along with it,' she said softly and Joe patted her hand, smiling.

'And you won't forget what I said about keeping a maid?'

'No, love. I'll bear it in mind. Thank you, Joe.'

And so she would. But the girls had been together for so long that it seemed cruel to separate them, yet the Marsdens certainly couldn't afford to keep two, without the income that the paying guests brought in. By the same token, there wasn't enough work for both if it was just the family at Sea View.

Edie turned the problem over and over in her mind. How could she choose? Ida was sturdy and willing, and picked up new ideas quickly. Quite often she and Edie seemed to come up with the same idea at the same time, which was another bonus. They would always work well together.

On the other hand, how would poor Minnie fare if she was turned out to fend for herself? Edie would make sure she found a new position, of course, but without Ida to look out for her she would probably be put upon, even bullied.

All this had already occurred to Ida.

'I don't think Madam is going to take in guests next season,' she confided to Minnie. 'She hasn't enjoyed it one bit, and it's not like she has to do it. She owns this place, and she has a husband to work for her. She's not in service or anything.'

Minnie looked at her friend fearfully. 'Then what do you s'pose will happen to us, Ida? She won't want us then. Where would we go? The orphanage won't have us back, not at our age.' Tears glistened in her eyes. 'What are we going to do, Ida? I like this job, I do.

I've been happy here.'

'Never you mind, Min. I'll take care of you. We'll find a job where we can go together.' Ida gave the smaller girl a hug. They would manage somehow — but it wasn't going to be easy.

Unknown to the two girls, their employer was still wrestling with the problem, thinking now that it might help if Flo would take one of the girls: that way they could stay near each other.

But there didn't seem to be any point in asking, when Flo had two girls of her own to assist her. On the other hand, Edie wasn't about to keep running Sea View as a guest-house just to accommodate two servants, however fond she was of them. Oh, dear, there had to be some solution to the problem!

Edie got to her feet, fumbling for her shoes. 'I'll go next door and have a word with our Flo,' she told herself. 'She'll know what to do.'

'A Toast!'

Florence clapped her hands together in glee. 'I can't tell you how glad I am that you've decided to stay, Edie. I was so afraid you'd pack it in and move back to Leamington. What changed your mind?'

'It was Joe mainly. He likes it so much here and he says the sea air has done him a power of good. I think it's more than that though, though I wouldn't say so to him. I think it's having a job he's able to do. You know that wasn't always the case before we came to Caxton.'

'That would help, of course. Men don't like to think they can't support their families. If it wasn't for you taking in washing back then I can't imagine how you'd have managed.'

'It was an uphill battle at times, but we survived. I didn't realise until now, though, that Joe understood how hard it was on me.' Edie smiled gently. 'Now he's offered to let me keep one of my little orphan girls as a maid.'

'What do you mean, one? How will you manage with just one maid?' Florence demanded. 'Even with two of them helping, you've been rushed off your feet at times.'

'Oh, didn't I say? We're staying in Caxton, yes, but I'm giving up the business.' Edie looked happy. 'With Joe working, and Bertie as well if he can find something, I'll be able to stay at home, but, of course, we'll neither need nor be able to afford both girls.'

'So who stays and who goes?' Flo asked in a hushed tone.

Edie put her head in her hands. 'That's my problem, Flo. I can't decide. I don't *want* to decide. I've racked my brains till I can't think straight, but I have no idea what the answer is! I thought perhaps you might suggest something. Any ideas?'

'Well, I suppose you could start

taking in washing again, or sewing?' Florence suggested.

'Not on your life. I've had it with that!'

Florence laughed heartily. 'I didn't mean you, silly! Let the extra girl do it. She can stay under your roof and work for her keep in that way.'

Edie wrinkled her nose. 'I don't want to turn Sea View into a glorified laundry. Got any more ideas?'

'Could you let the girl go out to work by day, but stay at your house? The pair of them wouldn't be parted then.'

'That's better, Flo, but I still don't know. I'd still only be dispensing charity and they're a proud little pair. They probably wouldn't care for that.'

'Well, I don't know. What about you? Do you really want to be a lady of leisure?' Florence asked. 'I can't see you lying on a sofa all day, twiddling your thumbs. You'll have to go to evening classes just to make the time pass.'

'No fear! I'm not going back to school at my age!' Edie chuckled. 'But I won't be a lady of leisure either, Flo. I mean, it wouldn't work, would it? Real ladies go to tea parties and call on each other with printed cards. I'm the wife of an assistant stationmaster. I wouldn't fit in with those lah-de-dah types.'

'I give up!' Florence laughed. 'You've said no to everything I've suggested so far. What you want doesn't exist; something which brings money in yet allows you to keep the house to yourselves. It's too bad you're not an artist — then you could paint pictures and sell them to your heart's content, to summer visitors who don't know Constable and his paintings from the monkeys at the zoo.'

To her surprise, Edie jumped to her feet, a delighted look on her face.

'That's it!' she cried. 'You've given me a wonderful idea. That's what I'm going to do!'

Florence let out a shriek. 'No, Edie, no! I was only joking. I never thought you'd take me seriously. You've never so much as held a paint brush in your life.'

Edie laughed. 'And I don't want to now. Look, I've got to put my thinking cap on, and I'll have to speak to Joe first, but come round this evening and I'll tell you what I've decided.'

She hurried off, leaving her sister staring after her, bewildered.

★ ★ ★

Full of curiosity Florence and her daughters crowded into Edie's parlour that evening, joining her two wide-eyed housemaids. Joe was hovering in the background, beaming.

'Quiet, everybody! Now for the big announcement. I'm going to run a tea-room here!' said Edie, smiling broadly.

Florence looked at her in surprise. 'Are you sure? You'll still be working with awkward customers, you know.'

'Not in the same way. In a tea-room, they'll only be coming in during set hours, not staying for a week or two as the summer visitors have been doing.

'We'll use one downstairs room — perhaps two if it catches on — and keep the rest of the house for ourselves. I'll do the baking, which I'll enjoy, and Ida can be my waitress. Minnie stays on as housemaid.'

'No good me serving the teas, seeing as me hands is so clumsy,' Minnie announced cheerfully, 'and me and Ida still get to live together at Sea View. I think it's a wonderful idea that Madam had.'

'It *is* a wonderful idea!' Florence enthused. 'You could have a counter where you could sell extra baked goods, too. Ladies stopping in for tea could buy treats to take home for their families. And you could supply cakes and tarts for special customers, such as myself. I could serve them to my guests, couldn't I?'

Joe spoke up then, suggesting that his wife and sister-in-law should scour the second hand shops in search of small tables and suitable chairs, which he would renovate and paint up.

'And you must get special coloured tablecloths and napkins to go with the décor,' Alice put in.

'And I could make myself an apron to match, Madam,' Ida put in.

Minnie had become very quiet and Vicky suspected that she was feeling left out. After all, it wouldn't be much fun to be mopping and dusting upstairs while everybody was down below taking part in the new venture.

'You've all forgotten something,' she remarked.

'What's that, Vicky?'

'Well, who's going to take the customers' money?'

'Me. I can pop it in my apron pocket,' Ida declared.

'It won't look very professional if you have to keep fishing in your pocket for change, and you'll be running back and forth with loaded trays as well.' Vicky looked thoughtful. 'No, if you're only going to have limited opening hours, why can't Minnie be in charge of that side of things? You can provide her with a real cash box, or even a till if they're not too expensive.'

Minnie was pink with pleasure. 'And I could have a coloured apron, same as Ida!'

Edie had opened her mouth to veto the idea, but she quickly closed it again on seeing the little maid's joy. 'That's an excellent idea, Vicky,' she said quietly instead. 'Well done!'

'I don't want to be the only member of the family who isn't taking part,' Bertie piped up suddenly. 'Unless I get another job soon I'll have nothing to do until next summer when I work with the donkeys again. Can't I do something to help decorate the place?'

'You can help me paint the tables and chairs, son,' Joe told him. 'I'll be glad of your help, especially on wet days. You know how the damp gets into my muscles.'

So it seemed as if the plan would benefit everybody concerned. And as Edie remarked, since they already owned the house it wouldn't matter so much if the venture failed because they wouldn't have lost anything but a few sticks of renovated furniture. They already had lots of cups, saucers and plates, and even a few three-tier cake stands.

'Mum's sewing machine is in good working order,' Alice said. 'If you buy the material, Auntie, I'll run up the aprons and table napkins for you, if that would be of any use.'

'It certainly would, my girl. What a good idea, you being used to sewing and such.' Edie smiled. 'I'll go to the shops and see about getting the material.'

'And you'll need several aprons,' Florence warned, 'in case things get spilled and there isn't time to wash and dry them.'

'I've thought of another thing,' Alice put in. 'Just to save the nice tablecloths getting too dirty, why don't we make shorter white ones to partly cover them? That'll save a bit of work.'

'Excellent!' said Edie.

More ideas followed rapidly and their excited chatter went on long after midnight. It was a very happy family who eventually retired to bed at Sea View that night.

★ ★ ★

The two families were planning to spend Christmas together and when the great day came they all crowded into the parlour where trestle tables had been set up for their Christmas dinner. Vicky had suggested they had it in the conservatory, saying it would be more festive there with frost on the glass, but her mother vetoed her suggestion.

'Never mind festive — we'd freeze in there! We don't want to spend New Year in hospital with pneumonia! We'll have a fine fire in the parlour, like sensible people!'

Privately Vicky thought she wouldn't mind being in hospital if it was St Martha's in London! Then she could at least see Brian.

Since he'd left Caxton, they had exchanged letters regularly and it was the highlight of her day to receive an envelope addressed to her in Brian's sloping handwriting.

There was nothing lovey-dovey about those letters yet she cherished them and kept them all in a little wooden box on her dressing-table. He was good at describing things and she could imagine him sitting in his unheated little cell of a room, swathed in a blanket as he tried to digest the contents of Grey's Anatomy, a weighty tome which all students had to learn practically by heart.

Then there were the nights spent on the quiet wards, or in the bustle of Casualty.

On Christmas morning the Williams and Marsden families attended church together. Florence had put the turkey in the oven before leaving home.

As they made their way down the aisle of All Saints' Church Alice noticed Mona Carrington sitting beside her aunt. The old lady looked regal in her massive fur coat and hat, but disappointment seemed to have affected Mona so that somehow she appeared diminished in size.

Alice had hoped that the other girl had forgotten about Monty by now, but something was certainly upsetting her. Perhaps her aunt was becoming more demanding with age and was treating Mona like one of those downtrodden companions in Victorian novels. It certainly seemed a likely explanation for her dispirited appearance.

Alice hoped that one day, Mona would find the courage to do something to change her life.

★   ★   ★

As for Alice herself, she had a secret to hug to herself. She wouldn't be seeing Jack today because he'd gone to spend Christmas with his family. However, he had called on her on the morning of Christmas Eve, asking if he could have a word in private.

Florence had shown him into the conservatory. Alice might be well into her twenties but her mother was very much a product of the Victorian age and didn't believe in leaving daughters alone with a young man unchaperoned — especially after what had happened with Vicky!

The mansions of England might have well-heated conservatories filled with grape vines or tropical plants but the one at Stella Maris got the full blast of the winds off the sea, so if Jack had any thoughts of bestowing a Christmas kiss on Alice, he'd think again when their teeth were chattering.

'I can't stay long, Alice,' he said, 'but there's something I want to ask you before I go. You don't have to give me an answer now but I'll see you in the New Year and you can tell me then.'

'Yes, Jack, what is it?'

She waited expectantly.

He hesitated for a moment and then, swallowing hard, he sank to his knees and taking both of her hands in his, he gazed up at her.

'I love you, Alice, very much. In fact, I fell in love with you that very first time I saw you, at the Palais de Danse. Would you do me the honour of becoming my wife?'

A radiant smile spread over Alice's face. 'Of course I will!' she replied and for a long moment they remained like statues, frozen in time, before Alice came to her senses.

'You'd better get up before you catch your death on those cold tiles,' she remarked, and Jack scrambled to his feet, still clutching her hand.

'Shall we go and tell Mum and Dad?' she wondered, but he shook his head.

'Do you mind if we keep it to ourselves for just now?' he asked. 'The thing is, I'm saving up to buy you a ring, Alice, but I don't have enough money yet. Your birthday is in April, isn't it? I might have enough by then, and that's when we could make the announcement — when you've actually got something on your finger to show everyone.'

Alice nodded happily. She was quite agreeable to going along with his wishes. To think that she was actually going to be a married woman in the not-too-distant future! Of course, it might be some time before they could set the date as neither of them had anything to start married life on.

No matter. At that moment Alice would not have changed places with anyone in England, not even the King's sisters.

★ ★ ★

When they were all seated around the table on Christmas afternoon there was no happier person present than young Minnie. She had never seen such a feast and she looked from one dish to another with shining eyes. Roast potatoes, carrots, Brussels sprouts, bread sauce, dark brown gravy and more. There was a huge piece of succulent pork, covered in crackling and, glory of glories, an enormous golden turkey.

Minnie was almost too overjoyed to swallow her food. She spent a lot of time simply looking round at everyone seated at the table, with a warm, happy glow flowing through her.

All through her growing-up years she had dreamed of belonging to a real family. One day, she was sure, someone belonging to her would come to claim her saying that it had all been a mistake, she wasn't really a foundling after all. Or a beautiful lady would sweep into the matron's office, saying that she had always longed for a little girl to love, and Minnie was to come home with her.

Needless to say these dreams faded in time, but now, looking shyly round the table, she felt she belonged at last.

What a Christmas this had turned out to be — and what a future she had to look forward to, after all the worry that had preceded Madam's plan to turn Sea View into a tea room! She and

Ida wouldn't be split up after all — they'd both be staying in this lovely big house, among the people who had come to mean so much to them. Minnie could hardly wait for it all to begin!

Glancing around the table at her assembled family, Florence felt very pleased with life, although if she couldn't get upstairs and loosen her corsets before very much longer she might burst!

What a year this had been! England had never been so prosperous as it was now, in the reign of King Edward the Seventh. Quite ordinary people were able to afford a summer holiday nowadays, which was why guest houses such as Stella Maris had come into their own.

It had been quite different in her childhood, when the only holiday for children of their class had been the Sunday School treat when they had all been loaded on to a farm wagon and taken to a field a mile or two away from home to play games and run races.

'We must drink a toast!' Alf declared, standing up to fill everyone's glass with homemade dandelion wine.

'Not you though, Minnie!' Edie cried a protest. 'You'll get all tiddly and fall over!'

Flo's dandelion wine was well known for its potency.

'Leave the girl alone, Edie,' Joe said. 'A little sip won't hurt her. She's a right to drink to the future, same as us all.'

The assembled company stood.

'To the King!' Alf cried.

'To the King!' the others chorused.

'Here's to 1908!' Joe said, raising his glass again.

'To 1908!' was the chorus.

Everyone there had reason to look forward to the New Year with happy anticipation so they downed a mouthful or two with a will.

'And here's to Aunt Clara!' Florence cried. 'None of this would have been possible without her!'

'To Aunt Clara!'

'I feel all funny!' Minnie moaned suddenly, and the room rang with laughter. What a happy sound — what a wonderful feeling. It was good to be part of a family, all together under one roof while the winter winds howled outside.

THE END